TALES OF
THE WOLF

Also available in Large Print
by Lawrence Sanders:

The Fourth Deadly Sin
The Eighth Commandment

TALES OF THE WOLF

The Cases of Wolf Lannihan

Lawrence Sanders

G.K.HALL &CO.
Boston, Massachusetts
1987

Each of these stories first appeared in a slightly altered version in magazine format in 1968 and 1969.

Published in Large Print by arrangement with Bill Berger Associates.

G.K. Hall Large Print Book Series.

Set in 18 pt Plantin.

Library of Congress Cataloging in Publication Data

Sanders, Lawrence, 1920–
    Tales of the Wolf : the cases of Wolf Lannihan / Lawrence Sanders.
        p.   cm.—(G.K. Hall large print book series)
    "Large print"—T.p. verso.
    ISBN 0-8161-4289-0 (lg. print)
    1. Lannihan, Wolf (Fictitious character)—Fiction.   2. Detective and mystery stories, American.   3. Large type books.   I. title.
[PS3569.A5125T3   1987]
813'.54—dc19   87-16608

Contents

Manhattan after Dark

I was watching the guy but it was the woman who made the play. Her hand snaked into her purse and came out waving a dinky little .22. She was leveling on my family jewels when I reached her. It was no time for chivalry. I brought the hard edge of my hand down on her wrist and heard the bone crack as the pistol thumped to the floor. A backhanded slap knocked her across the sofa into a cold fireplace.

Then the guy was down on his knees beside her, cradling her head in his arms.

"Stella," he crooned, "Stella, darling, it's all my fault. I'll take all the blame, Stella."

It was a nice try but it wouldn't wash. I had the caper cold and they were both in on it. Here's how they worked it:

They insured their run-down house for 100 grand, paying hefty premiums. He devised a firebomb, wired to the telephone, that was fixed to go off when someone called. The two of them left for a weekend at a beach motel 500 miles away. They made sure they were seen by plenty of witnesses. Then she slipped into a public phone booth in a drugstore and called their empty house.

It worked perfectly. The gas-soaked waste caught fire from the telephone dingus and the house was a total wreck. They thought they'd have nothing to do but collect the 100 G's.

But insurance companies don't work that way. Most of them are clients of the International Insurance Investigators (an agency known to the trade as the Triple-I). We provide the operatives and the investigation that makes certain everything is copasetic before the check is signed.

I was sent down from our Manhattan home office to look things over. It was easy to smell the gas soaked into the charred wood. The only thing that puzzled me was how they set it when they were 500 miles away. Then I found out he was an electronics bug, and I went over the telephone company records just on a hunch. It was a small town, and they had kept a written record of an uncompleted long-distance call. I braced them, blondie went for her little heater, and hubby cracked wide open when he saw her lying unconscious on the floor. I think the poor slob really loved her.

I dumped my evidence and suspects in the local DA's lap, then drove back to Manhattan that night. I was feeling pretty good. I had cracked it in three days and figured that Lt. Gen. Lemuel K. Davidson, USMC (Ret.), top dog at the Triple-I, might come across with a week off, with pay. What he came across with was a job that almost sent me to the Big Icebox in the Sky, with a red tag tied to my toe.

"Well done," he growled, in his best "damn-the-torpedoes" style. "Now this next one is something different. It involves a hotel B&E."

I knew he meant "Breaking and Entering," and I waited patiently for more details.

"This retired financier and his wife went to an afternoon matinee," he continued in his raspy, "chin-in, shoulders-back" voice. "When they returned to their hotel suite, the woman's jewels were gone. The door lock was forced. No one in the hotel heard or saw a thing."

"What's the tab?" I sighed.

He looked at me a long moment, then rocked back in his swivel chair.

"Nine hundred thousand dollars," he said.

I whistled.

He slid a printed list across his desk to me.

"There it is—diamonds, rubies, pearls, emeralds. I'm quite aware that you've been working rather steadily the last few years, Lannihan, and I assure you that once you've investigated this matter in your usual thorough manner, I shall do everything in my power to obtain a suitable vacation or leave-of-absence with pay for you."

Well, that's the way the guy talked. After all, he was a retired Marine Corps general—so who expected plain English? I took his list of the stolen gems, a PIR (Preliminary Investigation Report) from the New York cops and a Xerox copy of the policy with the Metro Insurance Agency, and I went back to my miniaturized office, took a belt from a pint of Jim Beam I keep in the bottom drawer and started reading up on the case.

The hotel was on Park Avenue, above 59th Street. The insured were Mr. and Mrs. Jules K. Alexander who were stopping in Manhattan for a few weeks before their annual pilgrimage to the French Riviera. They had a suite on the tenth floor, fronting on Park Avenue.

I contacted the hotel manager, a fussy little twit with a hairline mustache. He phoned the Alexander suite, and I went up. Even in the hallway you could hear the blast of the radio, the volume turned all the way up. Someone was playing a rumba and singing along with the vocal.

Jules K. Alexander was a fat, tycoon-type guy with a long cigar and a short temper. He screamed into the bedroom for his wife to knock off the damned radio so he could hear himself think. She didn't switch it off but at least she turned the volume down to a point where the windows stopped rattling.

Alexander told me that he and his wife had tickets for a matinee at a Broadway theatre. As far as he remembered, no one knew they were going. The jewels were locked in a strongbox hidden on the top shelf of the bedroom closet. He thought the hall door was locked when they left, though his wife was the last one out. They were in the lobby when she discovered she had forgotten her gloves and went back upstairs for them.

When they returned from the theatre, they found the hall door was open. It bore obvious signs of jimmying. The strongbox containing the jewels was gone. Nothing else had been touched, including some furs and

5

cheap costume jewelry left on the bedroom dresser.

I asked if I could speak to Mrs. Alexander.

"Ethel!" J. K. screamed. "Get your tail in here!"

She strolled in from the bedroom, and I caught my breath. A tall Alcoa-blonde poured into a black satin sheath so tight it looked like it had been sprayed on her. Her breasts were *there*, and the skirt was slit high enough to give me a glimpse of smooth, tanned thigh. Her eyes were heavy-lidded and the sullen mouth half-puckered. She lifted an arm to throw her long hair back from her neck, and the satin across her chest tightened and shimmered. She looked at me and smiled lazily. She wasn't wearing a thing under that dress. I knew it. She knew I knew it. I knew she knew I knew it. But this could go on forever . . . She spoke in a husky drawl, moving her feet about in time to the mambo rhythm coming from the bedroom radio. There was little she could add to what her husband had told me. Yes, she had locked the hall door after she had gone upstairs for her gloves. Yes, she frequently went to nightclubs. Yes, she frequently wore her jewels in public. That's what they were for, wasn't it? No, she hadn't been followed lately as far as she knew. No, she hadn't noticed any suspicious strangers prowling around. She smiled at me.

She smiled at me but it didn't catch. I didn't like the smell of this setup. She didn't act like a woman who'd just lost all her jewels. She acted like a happy woman, a relieved woman. It just didn't wash.

I thanked the Alexanders, examined the windows and doors and left. I knew the cops had dusted the place for prints and found nothing. A new lock had been installed on the hall door but the wood still bore the scars of jimmying. An amateurish job. I can open 90 percent of all locked doors with a plastic credit card and a gentle kick. So can most professional jewel thieves.

I left the hotel and went back to my office. I took out my pint of Jim Beam, kicked off my shoes, slid down in my swivel chair and started telephoning. I called every stoolie, hustler, fence, poolroom operator, bookie and pawnshop owner I knew. I passed the word all over Manhattan: the Triple-I was willing to pay $180,000 for the return of the Alexander jewels, no questions asked.

Legal? I guess not—but that's the way most insurance companies operate, and the cops hate it. We know the thieves will be lucky to get 10 percent of what the ice is worth from a fence. We offer 20 percent. The cruds make a profit and we shell out only one-fifth of what our clients would have to pay on the insurance.

So I put the word out that I was open for bargaining. It didn't take long. I came back from lunch and Miss Bazooms at the switchboard told me a guy speaking with a foreign accent had called and would call back. He did. It was Manuel Lopez, a small-time hoodlum in East Harlem. He wanted to meet me to talk about "an interesting shipment of goods" he had just received. I made a date to meet him uptown at midnight. Things were looking up.

I waited until evening, then went back to the Alexanders' hotel. The night shift was just coming on. I slipped a bill to the tenth-floor chambermaid, and we stepped out onto the fire escape for a little chat. She was a big, bosomy Swede with hips that bulged her starched white uniform. It was a small fire escape and she was jammed up tight against me. She didn't seem to mind it a bit—especially after I gave her the 20 bucks and let her see there was more where that came from. I patted her fanny tentatively and she giggled. It was hard to keep my mind on my job.

She had something interesting to tell me. A week ago she had been cleaning up in the tenth-floor corridor and had seen Mrs. Alexander running to her room from the elevator. Mrs. Alexander was crying, her dress was torn and there were big black-and-blue bruises on her bare arms and shoulders. She also had a mouse under her left eye.

I thanked Helga and told her she had been a big help. She asked if there was anything else I needed. I said there was—but daddy told me I wasn't old enough yet. She giggled again. I gave her another friendly pat that started at her shoulder and slid off her hip. It's amazing what 20 bucks will buy in Manhattan.

I walked over to a Third Avenue pub, ordered a double Jim Beam and took it to a dim booth to think things over. A few facts tied together and might mean something, or might not. Mrs. Alexander was a Latin-American music bug. It was a Cuban who phoned me. Might be something there. Then there was that jimmied door. That looked like an amateur. But the cheap costume jewelry in plain sight on the dresser hadn't been touched. That looked like a professional jewel thief who knew exactly what he was looking for.

I called the office and told the night man to get me a photo of Mrs. Alexander. He said that would be easy; she had been a lingerie model when she was unmarried Ethel Burgess, and there were plenty of hot cheese-cake shots of her around town. I also told him to have our Records Department get copies of the Alexanders' bank statements for the past year. Then I took a cab up to East Harlem to meet Manuel Lopez.

He was a greasy little crumb who wore elevator shoes and smelled of sardines. We sat in the back room of a Spanish grocery store and drank rot-gut rum. He had a "client" for me. The client wanted $300,000. I got up to leave.

"Make it 250 G's," Lopez said hurriedly.

"Make it 180," I said.

"Make it 240," Lopez said. He was beginning to sweat.

I got him down to $200,000 and then he balked. He bragged that he was representing "big men." He opened his coat and let me get a look at the sheath knife he wore under his left arm. He said he was "one tough boy." He said if I knew what was good for me I'd make the deal for 200 G's and not *uno centavo* less.

I told him I'd present the offer to my

company, and he gave me a number where I could reach him at certain times during the day. I knew it was a public phone booth. I shook hands with him when I left. I went home and took a hot shower.

I spent the next morning going over the Alexanders' bank statements for the past year. Jules wasn't in any danger of going to the poor house, but there was nothing wrong in his records. The personal checking account of his juicy wife was something else again.

There were the usual deposits and withdrawals of odd sums, but for the last seven months the record showed a cash withdrawal of $3,000 on the first of every month. In my lousy business, regular cash withdrawals of that kind of bread add up to only one thing—blackmail.

I must admit I leered when I flipped through the stack of glossy photos of Ethel Alexander the Records Department sent up. They were worth leering over. They showed her in evening gown, in bra-and-panties, in bikini, and one was just Mrs. Alexander—nothing else. She really had it—long, supple body with high, firm breasts, slender hips, smooth legs and the kind of creamy skin that

11

makes you think of—well, what the hell, it makes you think, that's all.

I waited till late afternoon, then started the rounds of Manhattan bars and nightclubs featuring Latin-American music. My act was the same in all of them: I flashed my potsy, didn't wait for the bartender to ask if it was a cop's badge or something that said "Garter Inspector," then showed a photo of Mrs. Alexander. I hit paydirt at the fifth place I visited, the Casa Mambo. The bartender knew her all right; she was in almost every night.

A few sawbucks opened him up a little more. He said she had fallen hard for a flamenco dancer named Rodriguez Garcia, a tough hombre who had a record as a knife fighter. Seemed like this case was full of knives, all sharp. I don't like the steel. Scares me more than a heater.

It took me until late at night to reach Manuel Lopez. I told him I had come across some information his "client" might find interesting. We made a date to meet on a corner on Central Park West in the upper 90s. I went home and got my piece, a .38 S&W Chief Special in a shoulder rig. Modest but effective. Lopez was waiting for me when I got uptown.

I let him gabble on about what a big man his client was, and how tough he could be, and what might happen to me if I didn't behave. I waited until we were walking through a shadowed section of Central Park West. Then I turned suddenly, grabbed a double handful of Lopez' wide lapels, lifted him a few inches off the sidewalk and slammed him back against the stone wall. I shook him until his teeth rattled, and his eyeballs began to roll around like agates. To tell you the truth, I was scared as hell.

"You cheap crud," I hissed. "You think you're talking to one of your crumbum pals? I ought to cut your tongue out right now."

I talked to him hard and fast, telling him what I knew and guessing at what I didn't. I told him I figured his client was Rodriguez Garcia. That somehow the Casa Mambo dancer had a hold on Mrs. Alexander and was clipping her for three big ones every month. That the pretty boy had gotten tired of the puny payoff and had made the lush chick finger her own jewels for him, after beating her up a few weeks ago. That Mrs. Alexander had gone upstairs after deliberately forgetting her gloves, and had left the hall door of the Alexander hotel suite unlocked for Garcia, or for one of his pals—

13

maybe for Lopez himself. That whoever pinched the ice hacked up the outside door to make it look like an ordinary Breaking & Entering.

Lopez didn't say a thing, just sucking the air into his lungs in a funny kind of wheeze and glaring at me with murderous eyes. I figured I had the whole caper cold. I told him he and his client could turn over the rocks, take the $180,000 and get the hell out of town. If they held me up for any more, I'd blow the whistle on them. What I didn't tell him was that I couldn't prove a thing I was saying. But I didn't have to admit that. He nodded his head—yes, they'd take the 180 G's.

I released him and he almost collapsed on the sidewalk. Then he straightened slowly, rubbing the back of his neck. His hand came away from his collar, and I caught a glint of steel in the dim glow from a streetlight. I turned sideways but I wasn't quick enough. I heard a *wheesh* as he sliced my right arm open from shoulder to elbow. It hurt like hell.

He knew about knives all right. He held it palm up, like a guy holding a key, and crouched, circling me. I couldn't bend my slashed arm to get into my shoulder harness.

All I could do was retreat warily and watch for an opening.

He feinted for my throat, and when I threw up my left arm he drove the blade for my ribs. I bent far to the right, brought up my knee into his groin and let him charge right into it. His scream of anguish must have alerted every cop in Central Park.

He went down on his back, vomiting, half bent over, holding his guts. I used my feet on him, breathing steadily through my nose and not wasting wind by talking. I took him in the kidneys, the belly, the groin, then the head and the face. I really did a job on him, using my steel heel plates when I worked over his eyes and mouth. That fink wouldn't be popular around the mambo joints for a long time to come.

He finally went out and I stopped kicking him. My knees felt weak and I sat down suddenly on the curb. I was still sitting there, trying not to be sick, when the first cop ran up, blowing his whistle like it was New Year's Eve.

It took 15 stitches to sew up my arm and four hours of steady talking to convince the cops that Lopez had gone for me because I refused to make a deal for the Alexander gems. The fuzz were suspicious but they had to buy my story. Lopez wasn't talking—and wouldn't until they dug his teeth out of his tonsils. I said nothing about the Casa Mambo or Rodriguez Garcia. He was my pigeon. I wanted him all to myself.

I awoke the next morning feeling like I had spent the night on the Penn Central tracks. My arm was aching, and I had the shakes so bad I had to drink my morning coffee out of a straw. I checked in at the office. General Davidson looked at my bum wing, grunted and asked if I wanted to be taken off the Alexander case.

"No, sir," I said.

"Carry on," he nodded, and I stood and resisted that terrible temptation to click my heels and salute.

Mr. Alexander had gone to work—or whatever it is that tycoon-type guys do for a living—when I got over to the hotel. That was okay with me; my business was with his wife, the ex-model. I phoned from the lobby and she told me to come right up. I could hear the radio blasting out a rumba.

She was wearing a black satin housecoat with red and green dragons embroidered all over it. It was slit up both sides so she wouldn't feel too bundled up, and it had a long zipper that ran down the front from neckline to hem. The zipper tab had a tiny silver whistle hanging from it. Cute, huh?

She asked me about my bandaged arm and I said I got it caught in a revolving door. She offered me a drink and I said I didn't drink before noon. She asked me if I'd mind if she had a little one. I said no. She had a little one.

"Would you mind turning the radio off for a moment?" I asked her.

She pouted but she flicked it off—which was, I remembered, more than she did for her husband. She coiled up in a soft chair and looked at me with those dopey eyes of hers. Her fingers played with the little whistle on the zipper.

"Mrs Alexander," I started, "how has Rodriguez Garcia been able to blackmail you for seven months and get you to finger your own jewels for him?"

I don't know what I expected—denials, tears, curses, bribes. I sure as hell didn't expect what happened. Her eyes opened wide, she uncoiled from the chair like a striking snake and came straight at me, her nails reaching for my eyes.

I had only one good arm but it was enough.

I sidestepped her lunge, tripped her as she went past and before she could recover her balance I had grabbed a handful of her soft, blonde hair and yanked back, hard—so hard the cords were standing out in her bent throat and her jaw was straining open. I pulled her close to me and I could smell the heat of her.

"Talk," I said.

She twisted around and clawed for my bum arm. I swung right around with her, keeping behind her, and punched a knee into the small of her back. She moaned. I tightened the hair grip again.

"Talk," I said.

She started to jab an elbow back at me, then suddenly all the fight went out of her. She collapsed on the floor, and I let her fall, releasing her hair. She began to cry, great racking sobs that shook her whole body. I sat down, had a cigarette and waited. She cried awhile, sniffling and wiping the back of her hand across her nose. It was very touching.

"Give me a drink," she begged, looking up at me through a tangled mat of hair.

"Talk first," I told her. "Then you can drink all you want."

"He took photos," she said. "Or a friend of his named Lopez took them. Or maybe he doped me. I don't remember."

"What kind of photos?"

She looked at me. "You know. Every-thing. They threatened to send them to my husband."

"You paid three grand a month for seven months?"

She nodded.

"It wasn't enough for them. They said if I helped them get the jewels it would be all over; they'd mail me the negatives."

"Did they?"

"Yes. I burned them."

I sighed. Negatives can be copied, and a couple of hoods like Lopez and Garcia prob-ably had thought of it.

"Where does this Garcia live?" I asked her.

She looked at me wildly. "I don't know. I swear I don't know. Maybe his partner knows. She's in love with him. Her name is Angela Diaz. She dances with him at the club. Maybe she knows where he lives."

I got to my feet. She was still lying in a heap on the floor. Her housecoat was hiked up around her thighs. Somehow—I'll never know how or when—the tab on the zipper had been pulled down. Way down. I enjoyed the view for a few minutes. She just lay there, staring at me, playing with the whistle on her zipper.

19

"What's the whistle for?" I asked her finally. She moved it slowly to her lips and ran a wet pink tongue slowly around the mouthpiece. "So you can find me in the dark," she whispered.

The toughest thing I've ever done in my life was turn my back on her and walk out of there.

I called the office and told the General about Garcia. He said he'd get men busy on it, and I went home to sleep. The office called me at 5:00. They hadn't been able to locate the dancer. Lopez was still unable to talk.

I took a cold shower, trying to hold my bandaged arm outside the curtain. I got dressed, slipping my .38 into my left coat pocket. It made a bulge, but it felt good, hanging heavy against my hip. I strapped a little leg holster against my left shin. It held a small, custom-built two-shot derringer. It was strictly a close-in gun, accurate to about 20 feet. But it packed a wallop. I headed for the Casa Mambo, driving my old Pontiac.

I had dinner there—something lousy with grease—then slipped the waiter five and asked for Angela Diaz. He said she might be backstage or she might not; her dancing partner hadn't shown up the last two nights. I asked him how to get backstage. He said it was against the rules. It took another five to repeal the rules.

Angela Diaz was sitting in front of the dressing room mirror, carefully plucking her eyebrows. She had yelled, "Come in!" when I knocked, but she was wearing only white bra-and-panties. She looked at me in the mirror and pulled up a dropped shoulder strap. That's what I like—a modest woman.

"I'm looking for Rodriguez Garcia, Miss Diaz," I said.

She went on with the plucking, not saying a word.

"I have some money for him," I added.

She swung around and gave me a disgusted look. "Cop!" she spat out.

"I'm no cop," I protested. "I work for Ethel Alexander. She sent me over with some money for Garcia. I'm to tell him it's all set. He and Ethel are supposed to catch the midnight plane to Mexico City. It's all arranged."

That hit her where it hurt. She stopped the eyebrow plucking, her jaw fell open and her face went red, then deathly pale.

"Mexico City?" she gasped.

"Sure," I nodded cheerfully. "Didn't he tell you? He and Ethel have it all arranged.

21

They've been planning it for weeks. They've got plenty of dough now. They're getting out of the country for keeps—together."

"You're lying!" she screamed.

I shrugged and wandered out the door. "Ask Garcia," I advised. "He'll tell you. You might tell him I have the dough for him. I'll hang around the bar here for a couple of hours."

I went through the bar in a hurry, ducked outside, got in my car and parked down the block from the backstage alley. I gave her five minutes. She was out in three, belting a polo coat over the bra-and-panties and tripping on her high heels. She took a cab. I was right behind. We went downtown, through Little Italy, over to the East Side. There was plenty of traffic; I don't think she spotted me.

She got out near Orchard Street, ran for half a block and darted up a narrow tenement staircase. I was right after her. She clattered up to the third floor. I heard a knock and a door opened, then slammed. I went more slowly. On the third floor I slid along from door to door until I heard a gabble of Spanish in 3-B—a woman's hysterical screech and a man's deep rumble.

I listened a moment. The voices went on

and on, getting louder. Then there was a scuffle, a short, throttled scream . . . and silence. I braced my back against the wall of the narrow hallway and kicked hard at the door of 3-B, just above the lock. It burst inward and I went in right on top of it.

Angela Diaz was down on the floor, her back propped against the wall. The polo coat was open, but the bra-and-panties were red now, red with blood. The hilt of a switch-blade was sticking out of her soft stomach. She curled her fingers around the handle but she had no strength to pull it out. Her eyes were puzzled as she watched her life flow down onto the cheap linoleum.

The guy had a coat on and there was a black suitcase by the kitchen table. He was small but quick, built like a steel whip. I went for the .38 in my pocket, slowly, awk-wardly, wondering why I hadn't drawn be-fore I came in, wondering if it was my last mistake.

He laughed, took one step toward me and buried his fist in my gut. As I caved over he brought his knee up hard and I felt my nose mash over my face with the sound of splin-tering bone. I had the stick out now but it wasn't doing me any good. I was down, my face in Angela's blood, and Garcia put a heel on the back of my hand and kicked the gun away. I pulled his legs from under him with my one good hand. He came down with a crash that shook the house.

He brought his knee up and I rolled in time to take it on my hip. I got a thumb in his eye, all the way, and his yelp of pain was sweet music. But he knew what to do. He pounded on my wounded arm and I felt the stitches pop open as a wave of warm darkness swept up from my toes, and finally my eyes clouded. I heard him scramble to his feet. Dimly I saw him grab up the black bag and start for the door. I took a deep, shuddering breath. I slid a hand down along my shin.

He was already through the door when I called, "Garcia," saying it softly, lovingly.

He turned, his eyes startled. His eyes looked at me, at my face. His eyes grew big as they traveled down to the little derringer I grasped tightly in my left hand. I propped my elbow on the floor and sighted slowly, carefully. His eyes pleaded.

I shot his eyes out.

"Well done," the General growled. "Very well done indeed. I think, in view of the circumstances, it would not be amiss to grant

you a two-week vacation, with pay, beginning immediately."

Two whole weeks, I marveled. What
would I do with myself? Then I remembered.

You know, that whistle really worked.

The Rogue Man

I had been on a Breaking & Entering that started with a jewel robbery in an East Side Manhattan hotel. It turned out to involve a particularly messy case of blackmail, and before it was over two people were dead. I broke it but I got a smashed schnozz and a knife wound in my right arm that slit me open from shoulder to elbow.

So Lt. Gen. Lemuel K. Davidson, USMC (Ret.), boss man at International Insurance Investigators, gave me two weeks off with pay. I had my nose reset by the company sawbones, drank a lot of Mr. J. Beam's bourbon and generally spent my sick-leave at this and that. "That" included some mild after-hours sport with the blackmail victim in the B&E case. But that's another story—and one you'll never see on these pages!

I got back to the Triple-I Manhattan headquarters on a Monday and spent two days getting caught up on my paper work. The General called me in on Wednesday morning and inquired politely after my health. I told him I was practically as good as new, and he nodded, shuffling a stack of papers on his desk.

Suddenly he looked up at me from under white brows that were as big and fuzzy as a Guardsman's mustache.

"You know Sam Barlow?" he demanded.

"Yes, sir, I know Sam. District manager in western Pennsylvania, Ohio and part of Kentucky. A good man. I've worked with him on a couple of things. Due for retirement soon, isn't he, sir?"

The Triple-I retires active operatives at 55. After that, the company figures, reactions slow down, the guy becomes hesitant about taking chances he should take, and the mortality-on-the job rate goes way up. So they pension us off at 55—if we're still alive at that age.

"Yes, he is," the General sighed. "In June of next year. But during the past three years, in Barlow's district, there have been 14 serious industrial fires. Six of our clients have been involved, paying out insurance that totaled more than $25 million."

"No evidence of arson?" I asked.

The General looked at me narrowly. "Barlow says not," he said—and let it hang there. I could hear a typewriter clacking in the outer office. I could hear traffic noises down on the street, 21 stories below, and I could even hear the hooting of a tugboat on the East River, three blocks over.

I remembered the night Sam and I went up against a wife-killer in a suburban house just outside of Pittsburgh. Sam took the front and I took the back. But the guy came out a side door we didn't even know existed. He circled around behind me, and I was a dead man until Sam came through the house like hell on wheels, a flashlight in one hand and his piece in the other. He put his light on the guy and fired almost in the same instant.

The guy went down, dead before he hit the ground, but his finger was still pumping the trigger of his magnum, and the slugs were throwing up dirt at my feet. It was that close. Yes, I remembered Sam Barlow.

General Davidson just looked at me shrewdly. He probably knew what I was thinking. The old bastard knew what everyone was thinking. That's why he sat in a plush Manhattan office and sent younger men out to die.

"You don't have to take this if you don't want it, Lannihan," he said gently.

I sighed, stood up and held out a hand for the sheaf of papers. The General straightened the file neatly and handed it over.

"Also," he added, "I am instructing Personnel to let you look over Barlow's personal file—if you so desire."

I nodded, did an about-face and got out of there. I may have slammed the door a little louder than necessary but that's the way I was feeling. Sam Barlow . . . my God, did the General really believe he'd go sour?

I went back to my cubbyhole office and took a long slug from the pint of Jim Beam I keep in the bottom drawer for just such emergencies. I called Personnel and asked them to send up Barlow's personal file. Then I dug into the reports on the industrial fires.

As the General had said, there had been 14 of them over the past three years. There didn't seem to be any particular pattern: they involved two paint and varnish manufacturers, an automobile tire recapper, two outfits that made farm machinery, a clothing manufacturer and other assorted factories. Two of the 14 were discovered to be in financial difficulties (a tip-off to arson) but the others were apparently in good shape.

Investigations by local fire officials and by Barlow's office didn't turn up anything either. There seemed to be some evidence of extreme heat in three of the fires. In one case the fire was hot enough to melt part of an engine block—but there was nothing conclusive or even puzzling—just 14 big industrial fires in a Triple-I district that usually averaged about two such fires a year. I knew the Mk. II computer in the Records Department had turned out a notice of the increase. That's how we work at the Triple-I; a machine tells us when things begin to smell.

There was a knock on my door and when I yelled, "Come in," a very leggy young person from Personnel popped in to put Barlow's file on my desk. Were miniskirts making a comeback?

"Hi, Mr. Lannihan," she breathed.

"Hi, sweetheart," I said. "Are your skirts getting shorter or are your legs getting longer?"

"Gee, I wish my legs would get longer," she said, looking down at them. "They're too short—don't you think?"

She stood with her knees together and looked up at me innocently. Innocently—hah!

"They're perfect," I said, "and you know

it. Now get your tail out of here before I fracture Interoffice Memo 341-B, titled 'Relations Between Male and Female Employees While on Office Premises.' "

"Oh *that*. No one pays any attention to that old thing." She swung about and her skirt flared up another couple of inches. Pink panties. Cute.

I spent two hours on Barlow's file. He was much man and it was a good record. Three serious wounds in line of duty. Plenty of big cases broken with arrests and convictions obtained. He was a college graduate with two years at law school. He had moved steadily up the Triple-I ladder, starting as a clerk in Records, transferring to Active Agents at his own request. He had been assistant manager in our Chicago office, then took over his present job about six years ago.

Four years ago his wife and teenage daughter had been killed in a car crash. I remembered sending him a letter of condolence and getting a nice thank-you note in return. We still exchanged Christmas cards.

There was absolutely nothing in his record to suggest he was anything but what I figured him for—a good, hard, conscientious operative, with as much moxie as any of us, and maybe a little more than most. I just couldn't see him going bad.

I called the General and suggested I go out to Barlow's office with a cover story that I was coming in as a replacement when Sam retired, and I was there for indoctrination and gradual shifting of the job load. The General agreed.

"Sir," I added, "I think he's clean as a whistle. I think it's a bad rap."

The General grunted and reminded me to file daily reports. He hung up first so I could slam the receiver down with some relief for my feelings and no danger to my future at the Triple-I.

Barlow's district headquarters were in a floor-through suite of offices in a skyscraper in downtown Pittsburgh. He was in the outer office, shuffling through a stack of mail, when I made my entrance, lugging my keister and briefcase. His face lighted up when he saw me.

"Lannihan the Wolf-Boy!" he shouted, rushing over to me with his paw out. "How the hell are you?"

We pumped hands and hit each other on the back and called each other "old bastard." He really seemed delighted to see me. He was a short guy, massive through the shoulders and chest, with a red face and a fine network of blue veins in his cheeks and nose that testified to all the good bourbon he had consumed in his lifetime. He was beginning to go to fat, but he still moved lightly on his feet and had a bone-crushing grip.

We went into his inner office, a pleasant layout with windows along two walls. The furniture was leather and comfortable. On the broad desk was a silver-framed photo of Sam's wife and daughter.

He brought out a bottle of sour mash and we each had a small one in paper cups. It was after 10:00 A.M. I wasn't surprised by the obvious absence of other agents; they could all be out on jobs. But I wondered why there had been no secretary in the outer office and why Sam had been about to open his own mail.

"What brings you to our bailiwick, Wolf?" Sam asked casually. "Just passing through . . . or you onto something down this way?"

I smiled at him. "You idiot," I said, "can't you guess? I'm your lousy replacement. You're over-the-hill, Sam, and they're farming you out. You know the drill: you'll break me in for six months and then go back to Manhattan to teach the new agents every-

thing you've learned in your illustrious career for the final months on salary."

For a moment he seemed shocked, his
features frozen. Then he relaxed and laughed
ruefully.

"I should have known," he said. "Wolf, I
swear I forgot all about it. Of course . . . I'm
down the drain next year. Well, baby, I'm
delighted it's you, and congratulations. We've
got a good setup here and I know you're
going to do a great job."

We had another bourbon on that and
started discussing how we'd handle the take-
over. We agreed Sam would keep his office
and desk until he moved back to Manhattan.
I'd move into a small outer office and work
on the "Cases Pending" files from there.
Sam would take me around to meet the
clients in the district, and I could go along
with all the four district agents on their investigations and see for myself how they
operated.

"They're young, Wolf," Sam said seri-
ously, "but they're all good men. One of
them, Fred Aikens, is a whiz. He's really
going places. But the first thing we've got to
do is get you settled."

I knew Sam owned a big house out toward
Allison Park, and I expected he'd ask me to

stay with him. It seemed the normal thing to do since he was rattling around out there alone, living a widower's life.

But he started talking about hotels, and I didn't say a word. We finally decided on the Concorde, and he suggested we lug my stuff over there and get me checked in. It was only a few blocks from the office.

We were on our feet, moving toward the office door, when it suddenly burst open, a young girl came rushing in and said, "Sam, darling, I'm sorry I'm late, but I just—"

She broke off suddenly when she saw me. "Oh, I'm sorry," she said, without missing a beat, "I didn't know you were busy."

Barlow handled it very well. "Come in, Judy, come in," he said. "This hunk of enfeebled manhood is your new boss, Wolf Lannihan, down from the home office to take over from me. Wolf, this delectable morsel is Judy Cummings, who runs the place. If you want to know anything about anything, just ask Judy."

The three of us chatted lightly about this and that, and I made certain that nothing in my voice or manner told them that I found it a mite unusual that the secretary of a Triple-I district manager would call her boss "darling" when she thought they were alone.

Nothing too awful about it, of course; still, I found it curious . . .

She was a little thing but well-machined with everything in abundance and in the right place. Beautifully dressed in grey silk, and I made a mental note to check her salary and the petty cash records. An amusing, pixieish face with very mobile features she was always twisting into grins and smiles and funny little frowns. She came on strong, like an actress. But I noticed her calm blue eyes didn't smile or frown. Her eyes had an existence of their own—wise and observant. No dumbbell, this chick, but she seemed to want to make the world believe she was.

I spent the first month latching onto the routine. Barlow and Judy Cummings ran a tight ship, and there wasn't a file I asked for that wasn't located and handed to me immediately. The four junior agents were disciplined, respectful and, as far as I could see, doing their jobs well. Fred Aikens, the kid Sam had mentioned, was a tall, gawky, freckle-faced lad with an engaging grin. What he lacked in looks he made up in brains and personal charm. I agreed with Sam's estimate: Aikens was destined for a successful career with Triple-I, if he lived.

Sam's "Open & Pending" file was surprisingly small for a district as large as his. There were the 14 industrial fires that, I noted in my first daily report to General Davidson, Sam was carrying as being of "undetermined but possibly suspicious origin." There was also a six-year-old case involving the death of a certain Dr. Leffert Greene, murdered by a "midnight prowler" during an apparently successful burglary. His heirs had collected $90,000 double indemnity. An exhaustive investigation by local police officials and by Barlow's office had uncovered no leads.

As I say, the first month was pure routine. I kept my nose clean, tried not to pry too much and made only a passing reference to the 14 industrial fires, a question that Sam answered calmly and completely. I asked him who in the office had been assigned to them. He said Aikens had handled the first three. Then, when there was a fourth, Sam took over the investigation personally, and he had checked out the other 11.

I wired Manhattan Records for a run-down on Fred Aikens, the other three agents and Judy Cummings. I had absolutely nothing to go on other than Sam's lack of hospitality in not asking me to share his digs while I was working out of his office. That and Judy

Cummings' "Sam, darling . . ." when she broke into the office that first day.

Hardly enough to hang anyone!

My relations with the office staff were good. Barlow and I had dinner together at least once a week and lunch almost every day that I wasn't in the field. At least twice the whole staff, including the luscious Judy, had a late dinner together and talked shop. I was beginning to appreciate that Cummings girl. The kittenish pose was just a come on; she really had ice water in her veins and a brain that never stopped ticking. She had sex all right, but knew when to project it and when to keep it under control.

I decided that, if she wanted to, she could make a man climb walls. I could imagine taking her to bed, but the dream didn't give me too much pleasure. I saw myself yelping and giggling with pleasure while she did everything I asked and watched me with those calm, dispassionate blue eyes. Not a pretty picture.

I had asked that the files requested from Manhattan Records be sent directly to my hotel suite, not the office. On the night they arrived I had a late dinner in the hotel grill, bought myself a fresh pint of Jim Beam for company and went upstairs to do some homework. I flicked on the bed light, kicked off my shoes, mixed a Mr. B.-and-water and tuned in some soft Gilbert and Sullivan on the hotel radio. All very cozy.

I went through the files on the four agents carefully. They were all clean—completely. I was amused to note that Fred Aikens was considered one of the nation's experts in three-dimensional chess—but other than that there was nothing suspicious!

Agents, of course, get a thorough check-out. Secretarial employees are investigated, too, but not in so much depth. The file on Judy Cummings ran only two pages. She was 26, had dropped out of college after two years and had, I was intrigued to read, a small brown mole under her left breast. It also said she had a brother, two years younger, who was presently serving with the U.S. Army.

It was the last sentence of the report that gave me the feeling I was suddenly being choked.

It said that Judy Cummings and her younger brother, Richard, were sole heirs of their stepfather, Dr. Leffert Greene, who had been murdered by that "midnight prowler" six years previously. The two, Judy and

Richard, had shared equally the $90,000 double-indemnity insurance payment.

I'm a dirty-minded, cynical slob, and I lay there in my bed in the Concorde Hotel in downtown Pittsburgh, and I wanted to cry. I live on the underside of the world—the shadowed side of violence and greed and lechery. The only thing that keeps me from being overwhelmed by the darkness is the friendship of guys like Sam Barlow. When the guy and the friendship go sour, a little of me has to die.

I knew then that, somehow, General Davidson was right; Barlow had gone bad. I sent a cable off to Manhattan Records, in the office code we sometimes use, asking for the answers to two questions. Then I sent down for another bottle of bourbon and tried very hard to get drunk. Instead, I got very sick, couldn't sleep, and didn't show up at the office the next morning. I called Judy to tell her I was dying—which wasn't much of an exaggeration—and that I'd be in after 1:00.

Suddenly I had a terrible yen to drink some super-iced champagne. I sent down for a bottle, made certain it was so cold it was tasteless, and downed the entire bottle almost as fast as I could gulp it. It brought me back to the land of the living where I dwelt for almost an hour when the telegram I was waiting for arrived. It answered my two questions.

Richard Cummings, Judy's brother, was a 1st Lieutenant in the Chemical Warfare branch of the U.S. Army. That had been a long shot—but it paid off. The other answer hurt even more.

Sam Barlow had collected $58,000, double indemnity, when his wife and daughter had died in that car crash four years ago.

I sat a moment, trying not to upchuck the champagne. Then I started a letter in longhand to General Davidson, asking that I be relieved of the assignment and another agent sent out. I had finished about half of it when I stopped, tore up what I had written and flushed the pieces down the toilet.

Dogging the job wouldn't do anyone any good—least of all me. I knew the General had seen copies of my wires, and he could put two and two together and come up with seven as easily as I could. I had to see this thing through—old Judas Iscariot Lannihan, the Wolf-Boy.

I had a lunch of something that tasted like tissue paper and dragged myself over to the office. I must have looked like death warmed over because Judy Cummings, at the front desk, smiled at me sympathetically.

"Too much drinkee?" she asked.

"Yeah, too goddamned much drinkee." I went into my office and slammed the door. I was properly grateful that Sam was out of town, lunching with a client.

I got the files out on those 14 industrial fires. This time I saw something I should have seen before. But I hadn't been looking for it and I missed it.

Remember I said that extreme heat had been noted in the reports on three of the fires. As I knew they would be, those were the first three fires—the ones investigated by Fred Aikens. When Sam Barlow took over the investigation of the fires personally, there was no more mention of extreme heat.

I slouched around to Aikens' office and fell into a chair alongside his desk. I asked him about the fires. He was properly cautious; it wasn't his case anymore. But after awhile he started opening up.

"After the first two fires, I started reading up on arson," he told me in his earnest eager-beaver manner. "I was convinced some super-hot chemical was used in those first three fires, the three I investigated."

"Any idea what it could have been?"

"No. Thermite maybe. Or one of the new plastic explosives the Army has developed. They got some stuff like napalm, you know, but more solid. About like a modeling clay. You can set it off with a cap, a fuse or a radio-controlled trigger. It explodes or burns hot as hell, depending on which type you use."

"Ever find any actual evidence it was used—or any other chemical?"

"No," he said regretfully, "I never found a thing. But Sam Barlow would know."

"Yeah," I said. "Sam would know."

I took the company car and drove out to the small suburb where Dr. Leffert Greene had been murdered six years previously. They were still carrying the case in their "Open" file. Judy Cummings and her brother Richard had returned from a party at midnight to find their stepfather bludgeoned to death in his study. Windows were broken, the house had been ransacked and a valuable collection of jade jewelry was missing. A neighbor thought she had seen a "mysterious stranger" prowling around. I wish I had a dollar for every time an imaginative neighbor has seen a "mysterious stranger" in a case like that.

I drove over to Barlow's village and

checked the vehicular casualty reports. His wife and daughter had driven into a bridge abutment at high speed. It was a clear, moonlit night, no rain, a well-lighted road with reflective signs. The cops never had figured out what went wrong. Neither mother nor daughter had been drinking; there was practically no traffic. I didn't ask them if anyone had tampered with the steering knuckle of the car. I knew they hadn't checked. Why should they?

I found a local tavern and put in a collect call to the New York office. I asked Records to find out exactly what kind of a job Lt. Richard Cummings had with Chemical Warfare. I told them to call me back at the phone booth of the tavern and gave them the number.

Four slugs of Jim Beam later the call came through. Cummings was doing research on plastic explosives; that's all the Army would say. It was enough.

The whiskey hadn't done me a bit of good. I knew I should take everything I had back to the home office, dump it in General Davidson's lap and let him take it from there. But I had known Sam too long; I had to give him a chance to convince me I was a stupid, suspicious, ungrateful crud out to hang a man who had once saved my life.

There were lights burning in Barlow's house, and I walked up the graveled driveway like a gallows was waiting for me inside. I rang the bell. Then, after a moment, I rang again.

"Who is it?" Sam's voice came from inside the locked door.

"Me, Sam. Lannihan. Can I see you for a minute?"

Nothing happened for a moment. I thought I heard whispering but I might have imagined it. Finally I heard a chain unlatched, a bolt twisted, and the door opened.

"Hey, boy," Sam Barlow said. "Come in, come in. Just in time for a nightcap or two or three."

We went into his comfortable living room. I slouched in a leather armchair, and Sam went over to a corner bar to pour some sour mash over rocks. While I was waiting for my drink I noted the lipstick-stained cigarette butt in the cocktail table ashtray. And I could smell her perfume. I figured she had gone into the kitchen or was upstairs. It didn't matter.

"Cheers," Sam said and held up his drink.

"Cheers," I said and drained almost half my glass in one gulp.

"Hey, baby," Sam laughed, flopping back on the couch, "take it easy. There's plenty more where that came from."

I leaned forward with my forearms resting on my knees, the drink clasped in both hands. I couldn't look him in the eye. But I listened to his voice.

"Sam," I said, "do you remember Al Devaney?"

"Devaney?" he said. "Devaney?" And I heard the note of caution come into his voice.

"Yeah, Sam. Al Devaney. He worked out of the LA office about ten years ago."

"Oh yes, sure, Wolf, I remember him. He went sour, didn't he?"

The voice told me—the deliberately light, casual voice, as phony as a three-dollar bill.

"That's right, Sam. Al went sour. He cooked up a crazy scheme with some dame. They tossed her husband off a train and tried to collect. Al was a smart boy—but not smart enough for that. Remember?"

"Yes," Sam Barlow said, and his voice was dull. "I remember."

"Why do you suppose he did it, Sam? Why do you suppose he tossed over his job,

46

his career, his wife and kids and made a stupid play like that. All for a floozy?"

I raised my eyes and looked at him then. Suddenly he looked ten years older, his features shrunken, his neck too small for his collar, his shoulders drooped and that barrel chest deflated.

"I don't know," he said slowly. "Maybe he loved the floozy. Maybe that's why he did it."

We must have stared at each other for at least two minutes, our eyes locked. Finally I could stand it no longer and looked away.

"Sam, Sam," I groaned. I felt like weeping. "Jesus Christ, Sam, why . . . *why?*"

He shrugged. "I'm not sure I know or understand. An old guy getting paunchy, ready to be put out to graze. Then a young girl comes along. A great body. Sex like it was when you were young. You see a way to start a new life. Just think, Wolf—a chance to begin all over again with a young wife, plenty of loot. Mexico, the Riviera, maybe an island somewhere. The hot sun. A chance to rest your feet. Fishing. I love to fish, you know. It seemed so easy, so easy . . ."

"Your idea or hers?"

"Half of each." He laughed bitterly. "We

were made for each other. We found each other."

He went over to the bar and poured us two more drinks.

"How long have you known?" he asked, not turning.

"A couple of days, I guess."

"What have you got, Wolf?"

"Nothing hard," I said. "You know how I work—all guesses."

"Yeah," he said. He smiled. "Educated guesses."

"I figure it started six, seven years ago," I said, taking the glass of bourbon from his outstretched hand. "Maybe she just happened to come to work for you. Her stepfather was the first. I figure you planned that. She and her brother did it, but you set it up. How did you hook Richard, Sam? Booze? Women? Greed?"

"Just the money," Sam said, "He's a playboy. AC-DC. A big spender."

"Then, when that one went off so sweet, it was your wife and kid's turn. I figure the steering gear in that one. You'd know how to do it."

"Yes," he said dully, "I knew how."

"Then, when Richard went into the Army and got assigned to Chemical Warfare, it was a whole new ball game. He told you about this plastic hotstuff he was working with. You saw a chance for big dough, and a lot of it. You probably hired local crumbums to do the placing but you supplied the material. That's how I'd have done it."

"You're smart, Wolf," he said admiringly, "you're really good."

"You made one little mistake when you had Fred Aikens investigate the first three fires. He sensed something was spoiled. You didn't think he'd be that bright. So you took him off the case and took over yourself. That's when the reports stopped mentioning a super-hot bomb or trigger, thermite or a plastic explosive."

"But listen, Wolf," he said eagerly, "you admit you've got nothing hard on us. It's all guesswork. You can't go into court with guesswork, Wolf. You know that. Maybe we can work a deal. How about that, Wolf? How about a deal?"

"Sam, Sam," I groaned, "will you use your goddamned brains? Fourteen fires. That means 14 separate deals with 14 factory own-ers for—how much? Half the take? So 14 guys are now involved in arson and fraud. And you mean none of those 14 are going to break when we lean on them? They'll crumble like cellophane straws. They'll sell you out so fast you won't have a prayer. No deal, Sam. It's fraud, arson and murder. Oh Jesus, Sam, you're dead. You're surely dead . . ."

"No," Judy Cummings said from the doorway. "No."

She was standing there in light blue bra-and-panties, her bare feet spread wide and braced on the polished wood floor. Her hair swirled down around her shoulders, and those cold blue eyes finally blazed.

I looked at that body—sugar and spice and everything nice—and then, finally, I could understand why he had done it, why he had gone off the rails. That body *was* a new life, new hopes and new dreams. I could understand what it meant to have that soft, pliant flesh beneath your hands and beneath your body, drawing youth and vitality from her like warming yourself before an open fire on a cold night. He couldn't resist that—and I wasn't sure that I could have resisted it.

But there she stood, half-naked and quivering, and in her hand was Sam's .38 Police Special. Sam got to his feet.

"No good, Judy," he said. "It's no good. The Triple-I has closed the case."

"But it's only him," she cried. "He's the

only one who knows. We can kill him and get rid of his body and you can—"

"Judy, Judy," he said softly, regretfully. "I tell you it's no good. If Wolf knows, then the General knows. What are we going to do—kill every agent they send down here? It's over, Judy. All over. We played it out and it didn't work."

I stood slowly, being careful not to make any sudden movements. I set my drink down slowly. I slowly straightened my shoulders.

"What were you going to do?" I asked, wanting to keep them talking. "How many more fires were you going to try?" I took a few little steps toward her. "How long did you think you could get away with it?"

"No more," Sam said. "We had one more planned, but after you came down I canceled. We were just going to wait for my retirement."

"What about me?" she said hotly. "What's going to happen to me?"

She swung her eyes and torso in his direction, and for a moment the muzzle swung off me. I figured it was the last chance I'd get and I made my break.

But he was waiting for it, and as fast as I was, he was faster. I had really forgotten how fast he could move. Under other conditions it would have been a delight to watch.

She saw me coming, swung and pulled the trigger. But he was in front of her by then and he took it. It caved him in and slammed him back, but before he fell he had just enough strength to swat the piece out of her hand. It skittered across the floor and banged into the wall. I got it before I turned to him. But all the action was over. It didn't last long. It didn't amount to much. But Sam Barlow was dying.

She was still standing there, the fire slowly seeping out of those blue eyes, leaving them once again cold, wise and observant.

I knelt at Sam's side but I couldn't do anything.

"I didn't want you to hurt her," he said. And he went.

I straightened slowly and took a deep breath.

"Listen," she said hurriedly, "maybe you and I can make a deal. Listen, Wolf, let's talk this over. Wolf? How about it? Let's talk it over, Wolf."

She started moving toward me, swinging her hips a little, jutting her breasts a little, her lips wet and trembling.

Then she must have seen the expression in

my eyes because her face congealed with fear and her mouth fell open.

"But . . ." she stammered, and it came out "b-but . . ." like a string of wet bubbles rising to her pale lips. "But you want to kill me, don't you?" she said, her voice hollow with dread. "Now, right this minute, you want to kill me."

"Oh yes," I said. "Oh yes indeed."

The Bloody Triangle

He was a court-appointed attorney for the defense—which too often means second-rate justice—but I liked him on sight. A chubby little guy with percolator-top glasses, his eyes bloodshot and weary behind the thick lenses. His office was as spotted and rumpled as the tweed suit he was wearing. There were law books, most of them open, scattered all over the place, and files of papers were sliding off chairs and the cracked leather couch.

I had persuaded his antique receptionist to take in my potsy, and he had promised to give me 15 minutes. His name was Nathan Palmer, and I found out later that he passed at least a dozen great job offers every year. He liked what he was doing: defending accused people who couldn't pay him. This is a life?

"What's your interest in this, Mr. Lannihan?" he asked, handing back my ID card across his littered desk.

"I don't know if you've heard of us, Mr. Palmer, but the Triple-I—"

"I've heard of you," he said. "International Insurance Investigators. Do claims investigations. Got some blue-ribbon insurance companies for clients. Got a good reputation."

"Thank you. Well, we—"

"You represent anyone in this Williams case?"

"Yes, sir. Thomas Williams was insured by Viking Assurance for 200 G's. Viking is one of our clients."

"Double indemnity?"

"That's right, Mr. Palmer."

"Well, I'm afraid Viking is going to have to pay out $400,000."

"You mean your client is guilty?"

"I didn't say that."

Here's how it went . . . and I'm telling you this from the files Viking had handed over to my boss, Lt. Gen. Lemuel K. Davidson, USMC (Ret.), who had promptly dumped the files into my lap.

Thomas Williams was a 38-year-old guy who could have spent the rest of his life yachting around Bermuda. I mean he had inherited that much loot. But he liked working, apparently, and started a management consultant firm after he got out of Harvard Business School. With his contacts, he couldn't miss. At the time of his murder, he was employing almost 100 people and clearing about 250 G's a year. He was a good-looking, athletic-type guy (I had seen his obit in the *Times*) who played squash and crewed in yacht races.

At the time of his death, he was beginning to run to beef and soften up a little—but don't we all? Five years ago he had married Susan Ann Foster of Roanoke, Virginia. From her photos, she appeared to be a tiny little slip of a thing, fragile and small-boned, with great lustrous eyes and the body of a young boy.

The Williamses bought an old townhouse down in Greenwich Village and sank a bundle into repairs and restoration. The townhouse next door, a twin of the Williamses', was owned by a brother and sister, Walter and Harriet Giles. They became friends of the Williamses. Good friends. Very good friends. In fact, there was plenty of evidence that Walter Giles and Susan Ann Williams were rubbing the bacon while Thomas Williams was off crewing on those Bermuda yacht races.

At 6:43 P.M. on the evening of April 24, Susan Ann Williams was up in her private bedroom on the third floor of the Williams house. She was putting the final touches on her makeup, she told the cops. Her husband was down in the first-floor living room, she said, fixing a shaker of martinis. They were going to have a drink together, then go uptown for dinner and the opera.

Susan Ann heard what she described as "a firecracker going off right there in the house." She hurried downstairs. The housekeeper/maid, who had her own apartment in the basement, came hurrying up. Together they found Thomas Williams lying on the floor of the living room in a pool of blood and spilled martinis (eight-to-one; very dry). He had been shot once through the heart. The gun that apparently killed him was lying on the rug, a few feet away. It had been fired twice. The cops later dug the second slug out of the wood paneling over the fireplace.

It took the cops about 24 hours to pin it on Walter Giles, the good, good friend who lived next door. As a matter of fact, the speed with which the New York cops worked was one of the puzzling things about the case. These were all rich people, and they had influence. Usually the cops move cautiously in cases like this.

Anyway, they got evidence of Walter Giles' affair with Susan Williams. They found Walter's prints on the gun. They established evidence that it was his gun; he had owned it for almost ten years. It was a dinky little .22 he used for plinking at his Maine cabin.

They braced him, and he wouldn't say a word . . . not a word. And he wouldn't get a lawyer. So the court appointed Nathan Palmer—which was why I was in his office. Got that all straight?

"But you think the widow's got a legitimate double-indemnity claim for 400 G's?" I pressed him.

He took off his glasses and rubbed his eyes wearily.

"I don't know what to think. Walter Giles won't talk to me. Oh, he'll *talk*—but nothing important. Did he or didn't he? Was it his gun or wasn't it? Were his prints on the gun? Where was he at the time of death? Was he in love with Susan Williams? Did he have sexual relations with her? These things he won't talk about."

I gave him a cigarette, we lighted up, blew

smoke up into the air and then looked at each other.

"I checked you out," I told him. "You've been around a long time. This isn't your first murder case. Everyone says you're a smart man. So tell me, smart man . . . did he do it?"

He sighed deeply.

"I don't think so," he said finally. "I got no evidence . . . no little shred . . . that says he *didn't*—but I don't think so. It's just a feeling I got."

"Can I talk to him?"

"Sure," he said tiredly. "Why not? I'll fix it up. If he talks—if he says *anything*—you'll tell me?"

"You'll be the first to know," I assured him.

Walter Giles was a tall, thin, pale guy with an undershot jaw and a weak mouth. They were still holding him because he had refused to make bail, though he probably could have paid it out of his pocket money. Nobody looks good in the clink, but this guy looked like he was shook, spooked.

Like Nathan Palmer told me, he would *talk*—but he wouldn't say anything of any importance. If the cops said the gun was his, then it was his. If they said his prints were on the gun, then they must have been. He didn't remember where he was at 6:43 P.M. on the evening of April 24.

"What about your relations with Susan Williams?" I asked him.

"I won't talk about that," he said, showing the first sign of force and determination I had noticed.

"Mr. Giles," I told him, "I've checked you out, and I know you and your sister come from a very good family. Surely you wouldn't want to do . . ."

But then I stopped, because something had happened to his face when I mentioned his sister. It's hard to explain; all I can say is that his face congealed . . . it froze right up. I looked at him for a long moment, then thanked him for his time, got up and left. I called Palmer and told him I had drawn a blank.

I went back to my broom-closet office, kicked off my shoes and poured myself a slug from my desk bottle of Jim Beam. It even tasted good in a paper cup. Then I called Records and asked them to round up every photo of Harriet Giles they could find. Then I got busy on my paper work and was still figuring new ways to chisel on the expense account when a messenger dumped a stack of black-and-white glossy photos on my desk.

Harriet Giles was in every one of them—and in 90 percent of them, so was a horse. This dame was very strong on horses. Hunt clubs. Riding at the shows. Her own racing stable for awhile. The whole bit. As a matter of fact, she looked a little like a horse herself—a long, masculine face with a nose that kind of hung down, hunched shoulders, a raw, powerful frame. I was thinking of entering her in a claiming race at Aqueduct when I noticed a caption on one of the photos. It started: "Harriet Giles—known to her friends as 'Harry'—is shown here . . ."

Harry. That was interesting.

I went to see the widow first, after calling very politely and setting up the interview. As usual, I said I was the investigator for the insurance company, it was all purely routine, but it was something that just had to be done before the $400,000 was paid. Her voice, on the phone, was southern, sweet and little-girlish. She was very cooperative.

She turned out to be just the nicest, sweetest, littlest ole southern gal you'd want to meet. Her skirt, legs crossed, revealed absolutely hairless, smooth, soft, tanned thighs,

61

and I tell you, bub, when she batted those pale blue eyes at me, I like to swooned.

Man, she came on as soft and sweet as a black pecan pie. In that low, lilting voice she told me all the horrible events of the evening when she found her murdered husband— "Ah tale you, Mr. Lannihan, ah lak to di-ed"—and she admitted (with much batting of eyelashes) that she and Walter Giles had been somewhat more than friends and neighbors.

"But ah sweah to you," she said earnestly, leaning forward far enough so that the neckline of her little ole black dress gaped invitingly, "ah sweah that nevah, nevah did ah believe Walter would be capable of an act of violence like that. It shocked me, Mr. Lannihan. Ah was truly shocked."

My God, she was good.

So I thanked her heartily and got a warm press of her little ole hand in mine—which seemed to linger just a bit. Then, floating in a fog of magnolia and mint juleps, I went home and made out a list of what I wanted to do:

   . . . have a 24-hour watch put on Harriet Giles.

   . . . have our Washington office check

out the family background of the widow, Susan Ann Williams.

. . . ask Lieutenant General Davidson to contact the precinct which handled the original run and try to find out how the cops had tumbled so quickly to the fact that the widow and the accused, Walter Giles, were playing house together.

It was just a guess . . . you know? It was a hunch. But any cop—whether he's a city homicide dick, a state trooper, FBI, CIA, Treasury, private eye—whatever—if he's got a feeling for his work, he begins to sense patterns. Sometimes—usually, in fact—it's got damned little to do with hard evidence and what will stand up in court. It's just a hunch he gets, a feeling for the pattern, a knowledge of what drives people and makes them do the things they do.

It's usually sex or money-greed, one or the other or both together. You've got to know people, what makes them tick, what makes them forget their fear of the law and punishment. It's got to be something strong.

While I was waiting for the reports I had requested to come in, I took one of the eight-hour shifts on Harriet Giles. I was on her two days, and she drove me batty. Canters through the park, a long visit to a Madison Avenue shop that sold nothing but polo equipment, another shopping trip to buy a riding crop in a downtown store that specialized in boots, jodhpurs and the like. This dame was nuts about nags!

Actually, it was Paul Simanowitz who came up with it. He had the midnight-to-eight shift, and his log for the third day recorded a meet of Harriet Giles and Susan Ann Williams. They went over to a dyke joint on the East Side, drank a bottle of wine, held hands . . . and I figured I was home free.

But it wasn't all that easy. I admit the reports helped. The General finally got the police information I wanted. They had learned about Walter Giles' affair with Susan Williams so quickly because she had volunteered the information. Almost immediately.

Our Washington office reported that Susan Ann wasn't really the wealthy daughter of the owner of a plantation festooned with Spanish moss, with faithful retainers singing spirituals in the slave cabins at night. As a matter of fact, Susan was the daughter of the town drunk (her mother had died at her birth) and was also known in her small birthplace near Roanoke as "Hot Pants"—and sometimes "Mountain Poon."

Our investigator added ironically that apparently it wasn't only boys that Susan Ann went for. She also had a strong affinity for girls, old men, snakes, doorknobs and cocker spaniels. An all-around girl . . .

I thought I knew what had happened—but I didn't know how.

What got me was the murder night itself. Susan Ann and the housekeeper/maid had both signed statements that they heard one shot, rushed to the first-floor living room and found the body of Thomas Williams. Still, the cops said two shots were fired, they had recovered one slug from the paneling.

So . . . who was lying?

Mrs. Clemson, the housekeeper/maid, was a dignified old black lady who wore a white, starched lace cap over her grey hair. Her basement apartment was so spotlessly clean it made me nervous—and more than a little ashamed of the pig-sty hotel room I live in.

She sat absolutely erect in a straight-back chair while I lolled in her one soft armchair and took her through the events of the murder night. She answered firmly and positively, and there was no doubt in my mind that she was telling the truth.

At about 6:15 P.M. that night, Mrs. Williams had asked her to go around the corner and buy a bottle of dry vermouth at the neighborhood liquor store. She had thought this a bit strange because she was sure there was an almost-full bottle of vermouth in the liquor cabinet.

But she had gone, returning about 6:30. Mrs. Williams had met her at the door, taken the vermouth from her, and told her that both she and her husband were going out shortly and would be gone until midnight at least. Mrs. Clemson then retired to her own apartment.

Hearing the shot, at about 6:40 or so, she pulled on a wrapper and climbed the stairs to the first-floor living room.

Now we came to the moment of truth.

"Tell me, Mrs. Clemson," I said, "and this is extremely important—did you arrive at the death scene before Mrs. Williams, or did you both arrive at about the same time, or did she arrive before you got there?"

"She was there when I got there," she said promptly and positively. "I'm an old woman and I got aches. It takes me time to climb those stairs. I went into the living room and she was there, staring down at poor Mr. Williams. She was saying, 'Oh my God, oh my God, oh my God,' over and over like that."

"And where was the gun?"

"Like I told the police—about three, four feet from Mr. Williams."

"Thank you, Mrs. Clemson," I said.

Suddenly her old face just collapsed, and she lowered her head, put a handkerchief to her nose. I could see tears well out of her eyes and streak down her cheeks.

"You know," she said, "Don't you, son?"

"Yes," I said, as gently as I could. "I know."

"The things people do," she sighed heavily. "The things people do."

I called Nathan Palmer and had him set up another meet for me with his client. I went to that room with the barred windows and laid it all out for Walter Giles.

"You were just the patsy," I told him. I know it was cruel, but I had to do it. "She endured you, but it was your sister she was after. She set you up. She got your gun—borrowed it or copped it, I don't know which. Anyway, it had your prints on it. So she sends Mrs. Clemson off on an errand about 6:15. Then she goes down to the living room and shoots her husband through the heart . . . bang, just like that. She probably came up close to him. She couldn't miss."

"Stop," he groaned. "Please stop."

"No," I said. "I won't stop. This is one cold cookie, and I don't like dames like that. So she waits for Mrs. Clemson to return with the vermouth. She takes it from her, and Mrs. Clemson goes back down to her apartment. Susan Ann waits awhile, then fires a shot into the woodwork. Maybe she's wearing gloves; maybe she's holding the barker carefully or smearing her prints. Anyway, it could be done. Easily. She tosses the gun onto the rug. The shot into the woodwork was the one Mrs. Clemson heard. She comes limping upstairs. Susan Ann is already there, crying, 'Oh my God, oh my God, oh my God.' Is that about the way you figured it? And wouldn't talk because the thought of this woman you loved—and who you thought loved you—having an affair with your sister was just more than you could take."

He just fell apart, collapsing in a puddle on the table, his head down on his folded arms.

"Oh my God, oh my God, oh my God," he said—like an echo. I was getting my fill of tears this day.

So I went back to Nathan Palmer's office and laid it all out for him. It would save the Triple-I's client 400 G's and get his client out of pokey, but I wasn't happy about it. And from his reaction, I began to think I was going to have another weeper on my hands.

He toyed with a letter opener, looking down at the desk.

"The things people do," he said.

And I remembered that Mrs. Clemson said it first.

The Man Who Didn't
Come Back

A county deputy, patrolling Beach Road in a squad car on the midnight–8:00 A.M. shift, found her. The imported car was parked on the sandy shoulder of the road. She was sitting farther down the dunes, closer to the sea. In the light of his flash, the deputy could see she was wearing some kooky kind of fishnet covering. She just sat there, a crazy pattern of black and white in the light he threw on her. Then he saw she was toying with a gun. She'd toss it aside, then pick it up and look at it, then let it rest in her lap awhile.

"It was scary," the deputy told me later. "So I unbuttoned my holster and took out my barker. What the hell; it was obvious she was shook. Something had spooked her."

"What are you doing out here, miss?" he asked her.

She looked up at him a moment with

blank eyes. Then her gaze turned seaward where a three-quarter moon was just beginning to come up out of the waves.

"He's gone," she said dully. "He said he was going to do it, and he did it. He just swam and swam. And then I couldn't see him anymore. And he never returned . . ."

The deputy took her in, and they finally got her story. She was Mrs. Martha Wallace, married to John Wallace, an investment adviser who had rented a big summer home just south of Indian Point. The Wallaces liked to spend their weekend afternoons and evenings on that long, deserted stretch of beach just south of Farmdale. The dunes roll for miles along there, with just a few summer cottages and beach shacks.

In the last few years a lot of things had gone sour for John Wallace, according to Martha's story to the cops. Their four-year-old son had died in agony from meningitis. A few months later, Martha's elderly father, suffering from an incurable cancer, had stuck his head in a stove out in Dayton, Ohio, and ended his pain the fast way.

And then a lot of John Wallace's investments began to go bad. Just a lot of lousy luck at one time, Martha said. The banks began to close in. The Wallaces lost their home in Larchmont and had to move into a smaller apartment. Some of the people in the Wallace office had to be let go—including a few that had been with him since he started.

All this misery piled on misery began to get to John Wallace, and in the last few months he had started talking about suicide. She tried to jolly him out of it, but it didn't work. He became more and more morose.

They rented the summer house at Indian Point with the little money her father had left her. On that particular Saturday, they had spent all day on the deserted dunes, swimming and sun-bathing, cooking hotdogs over a little fire they had made and drinking beer they had brought along in a cooler in the trunk of their car.

In the afternoon he had been fine—laughing and swimming and enjoying the food. Then, as night fell, John Wallace grew quieter and quieter. Finally he kissed his wife —"a funny kind of kiss," she told the cops— and told her he was going for a swim. She told him not to swim out too far; the surf was rising. John Wallace walked into the water and began swimming outward. She never saw him again.

"What were you doing with the gun?" the sheriff asked gently.

"It was dark." She shivered. "So dark. I didn't know what to do. I got the gun out of the glove compartment. John had a permit for it. Just having it made me feel better."

The sheriff nodded. He already knew the gun hadn't been fired, and he didn't think it was important.

"When the deputy found you, you were wearing sunglasses," he said to her. "After midnight?"

She looked at him strangely. "Sunglasses?" she said dully. "I suppose so. I kept putting them on and taking them off. I'm afraid I wasn't thinking very clearly."

The sheriff nodded understandingly.

However, Mrs. Martha Wallace was thinking a little more clearly about two weeks later when she applied for the $250,000 life insurance policy her husband carried. She was listed as sole beneficiary. The company was Chalon Indemnity. Chalon is a relatively small outfit with a two-man Claims Department. But they're one of the clients of International Insurance Investigators, the outfit I work for. We provide our insurance agency clients with the muscle and manpower for claims investigations when they can't handle it themselves. I drew the Wallace job.

The first guy I talked to was the deputy

who had found Martha Wallace sitting on the dunes, waiting for her hubby to swim back to her. Luke Appleby was a lanky, buck-toothed, freckle-faced lad—about 25 I guessed. I had read a copy of his report, but I went over it all with him again. There wasn't much he could add.

"How did she seem to you?" I asked,

"Loopy," he said promptly. "Real shook up. She wasn't thinking straight or acting straight. I guess that business with the gun and the sunglasses proves that."

"Mmm. How did you take her in, Luke?"

"In my squad car. Later I drove out with Mike Brodsky, and he drove her car back to town."

"Listen, Luke, when you saw her for the first time, when you got ready to bring her in, you didn't happen to feel the hood of the Wallace car, did you?"

"Sure I did." He grinned at me, and I could have kissed him. There was a brain under that mop of red hair.

"And . . . ?"

"Warm. Almost hot. But it would be after standing out in the hot sun all day."

"Kid," I told him, "if you're ever looking for a job, give me a call at the Triple-I. Maybe we can use you."

"I might just do that," he said.

I nodded, smiled at him and started away. But he called me back.

"Mr. Lannihan," he said earnestly, "there's something else, I don't suppose it means anything, but still . . ."

"What?"

"After I felt the hood of the Wallace car, and it was warm, I lifted the hood and felt the engine block. It was halfway between warm and hot. This is just a personal opinion, mind you, and I got no court evidence. But I'd say the block was hotter than it should have been, even for a car standing in the hot sun all day. I'd say that car had been driven about an hour or so before I found it."

I shook his hand. "Luke," I said admiringly, "you're a wonder."

After the Wallaces' kid died and they lost their home, they had to fire Mrs. Evelyn McWalash, a 56-year-old combination housekeeper and nurse they had employed for almost six years. I finally located Mrs. McWalash working in a candy store. I was hoping to get her to talk.

Talk? I couldn't shut her up. I made notes as fast as I could, but I had to spend all evening trying to make sense out of them.

She had the voice of a long-playing record played at high speed, a kind of Donald Duck quack that went on and on. Anyway I got a few things out of her that might or might not be important.

It was true John Wallace had been depressed after the death of his son, but she had never heard him speak about suicide. But she had heard him discuss his business troubles many times at the dinner table. She thought he might be going broke, and she had already located the candy store job before she was let go.

The bad luck of the Wallaces had an effect on Martha Wallace as well. She had always been the best of wives—"A saint, that woman, a saint, I tell you!"—but in the last year it had all changed. Men called during the day, and Martha always grabbed the phone from Mrs. McWalash's hand, and then said later it was the butcher, or a salesman, or an old school friend.

Also, Mrs. McWalash happened to know, Martha Wallace had been seen sitting in a red convertible with an unknown man, The car was parked on a dirt road in the woods just outside Huntington.

I called Lt. Gen. Lemuel K. Davidson, USMC (Ret.), boss of the Triple-I, and suggested he tell Chalon Indemnity to stall on Mrs. Wallace's claim, even if it meant a court case.

"Got anything?" he growled.

"Too much," I assured him. "Boyfriends. A red convertible. A gun that wasn't fired. An engine block that might or might not have been hot. A man and wife depressed and apparently breaking up. I got a soap opera, is what I got."

"What's your next step?" he asked in that voice of his which always reminds me of a dull saw going through raw wood.

"An interview with the bereaved widow, I guess," I sighed. "I've been putting it off, but it's time."

"Carry on," he grated, in his best Gyrene manner, and hung up with a click that left my ear ringing.

I'd guess her about 34–35. That was her age, not her bust measurement. *That* had to be 39–40, and yummy. The rest of her was just as delectable. A tall, dark woman who carried herself well, wide shoulders held back (to support that weight in front?), a straight spine, the easy walk and movements of a woman who took care of herself: plenty of swimming and tennis, facials and massages, exercise in the privacy of her bedroom every morning. And she smelled nice, too.

I invited her to dinner at Ribaldo's on the Island, and as she walked toward the table where I was sitting, she took off her dark sunglasses and smiled at me. That smile wouldn't melt steel—not quite. As I rose, I noticed she was only an inch or two shorter than I am—and I nudge six feet. A heavy woman, but she carried it like a teenybopper. She was wearing a simple linen shift of bright yellow, with very thin spaghetti straps. The skin of her bare shoulders and bare legs was smooth and tanned. Suddenly I could understand the boyfriend in the red convertible, parked on a deserted road.

I explained that the insurance investigation was purely routine, and I'd appreciate it if she could help me by answering a few questions. She nodded helpfully and understandingly.

We talked while we ate, and I was bemused to note that her grief didn't keep her from tucking away two extra-dry martinis, a giant shrimp cocktail, a one-pound sirloin (rare) and a baked potato that surely must have won first prize at the Idaho State Fair. She also managed fresh pineapple with kirsch for dessert, two cups of espresso and a pony of Rémy Martin. I kept up with her, and didn't have to start stifling the belches until we hit the dessert.

I took her through her story, point by point, and it was all exactly as she had reported in her interrogation by the sheriff and later by the claims man for Chalon. You think that was good for her? You're crazy. No one can tell the same story three different times exactly the same way. They use different words, or mix up the sequence of events. But she had it down letter-perfect.

Also, when she was speaking of how she waited for her husband to come back from his midnight swim, she said, "But he never returned." She had said the same thing to the sheriff and to the guy from Chalon. "But he never returned" is written language; it's not spoken language. If you were going to say it, you'd say, "But he never came back." Very rarely would any American use the word "returned" in that context. Maybe I was grabbing straws, but it sounded like a rehearsed speech to me—something that had been written out and memorized.

After her second cognac, I said, watching her closely, "You've been seen around with other men, Mrs. Wallace."

If I hoped to shock her or jolt her or make

her reveal something, I might as well have swatted Mt. Rushmore with a rubber balloon.

"That's true," she said calmly, looking into my eyes. "After my son died and John began to spend so many evenings in the city, trying to recoup his losses, I did start seeing other men. Luncheon dates and picnics. Things of that sort. John knew all about it and approved. I made no secret of it. Would you like their names?"

"Please," I said weakly.

"I have their addresses back at the house if you'll drive me home. I took a cab over."

So I drove her back to her apartment in my battered Pontiac. Naturally she invited me in.

"It'll only take a minute," she assured me. "I have their addresses in my desk. I hope it won't get the poor men in trouble. They were very kind to me when I needed it most."

"I'll be discreet," I promised her.

"Thank you."

But before she went to her desk, she switched on a dim light over a well-equipped corner bar.

"May I get you something?"

I spotted a bottle of Jim Beam, my plasma.

"Bourbon, please, with a little water."

I was interested to note that the ice bucket on the bar was already filled. Had she expected me to return with her—or was she expecting someone else?

She made the drink for me, then poured herself a dollop of Martel's Cordon Bleu. This dame knew how to live.

"Do you mind if I make myself comfortable?" she asked.

I couldn't believe it. I thought that cornball line went out with Myrna Loy and Ginger Rogers movies. I thought she was putting me on by quoting from every buckeye *Late, Late Show* I've ever seen. But no, she was serious, and went into the bedroom, leaving me nodding like an idiot, mouth open, eyes popping.

While she was gone I made a little bet with myself: If she came out of the bedroom wearing a sheer black negligee, I'd trade in my broken-down heap and put a $2,000 down payment on a new Nissan. If she came out wearing transparent nylon babydoll pajamas, I'd send $500 to my nutty brother in San Francisco. He thinks he's a poet.

She came out of the bedroom wearing the same yellow linen shift, with velvet mules on her feet.

"I had to get out of those shoes," she said. "They were killing me."

I almost cracked up with laughter. I laughed until my ribs hurt. She looked at me for a moment, puzzled, then smiled ironically. She got it.

"Sorry about that, chief," she murmured.

"My fault," I gasped, trying to stop laughing. "Please forgive me."

After that, things were on a much friendlier plane. She got me the names and addresses of her boyfriends from the desk, and when I got up to leave, she suggested I stay for another Jim Beam. It didn't take much urging.

If I had any silly idea about getting her polluted and revealing deep, dark secrets, I forgot it after the third drink. She matched me, cognac for bourbon, and her speech never slurred and her movements remained graceful and precise.

One movement I particularly admired. That was when she rose, walked across the room and plunked herself down in my lap.

"I like men," she told me.

"And I like women," I told her. "That gives us something in common right there."

She managed everything: leading me by the hand into the bedroom, unbuttoning and unzipping me, tucking me between the sheets, and then slipping out of her dress in one, practised wriggle.

She was everything I thought she would be—and more. She was big and warm and hungry and very appreciative. It all looked so good I didn't know where to start—but she showed me. What a splendid executive she was.

Her hair smelled faintly of the sea, and her flesh tasted faintly salty. Everything about her was warm and fresh, sun-stirred, as if she had been baking on a beach. She made a funny sound deep in her throat while I made love to her—a throbbing flutter that was like a cat's purr. Her whole body hardened and came erect, and I could grip the muscles beneath the smooth, hairless skin.

What an experienced woman she was! Clever and alert to every movement I made, she had a few new things she was delighted to show me and which I was happy to learn. We laughed, loved, drank, slept, staggered into the john occasionally, wrestled, tickled, loved, talked nonsense, slept, woke, loved . . . and at 5:00 A.M. the next morning I staggered out of there singing, "Come, All Ye Faithful"—and don't ask me why.

Fourteen hours of sleep later, I awoke in

my motel room, rolled over and called her. But no one answered. So I showered, dressed and checked out the three names she had given me—the three "innocent" boyfriends. And I remembered to be discreet.

One guy was her banker, one was her chiropodist (for God's sake!) and the third one owned a bar and restaurant in Glen Ford, about two miles from the Wallace apartment. The last gink owned a red convertible.

They all talked freely and told the same story. Yes they had taken Mrs. Wallace to lunch or an occasional party or picnic when her husband had to stay late in the city. It was all entirely innocent. (Having experienced the voracious appetites of Martha Wallace, I was inclined to doubt that.) But, quite frankly, I couldn't see any of the three as the boyfriend who would join with Martha in a kill-for-profit plot, knock off her husband and then sit back and wait for the insurance company to pay off. And until the corpse floated ashore, they'd have a long wait!

Just for kicks I tailed the guy who owned the bar for almost two days. All I discovered was that he was cheating on his wife and had a girlfriend, definitely not Martha, stashed in a motel about ten miles away.

You might guess that my evening of fun-and-games with the grief-stricken widow made me a little less aggressive than I might have been in probing the case and investigating every lead. And you'd be right. I hated to think that warm, full-bodied, joyous woman was implicated in any campaign to knock off her husband and collect the loot.

Still, as I told myself no more than a hundred times a day, a job is a job. Maybe that's why I called Martha a few times until, one afternoon, she didn't answer. That's when I slipped into her apartment and planted a bug under her phone. I had had the equipment sent out by the Triple-I headquarters in Manhattan, and it was beautiful.

There was a pick-up and transmitter no larger than a flat matchbox that fitted neatly inside the base plate on her phone. The range was almost 200 yards, which allowed me to park my hired Ford around the corner from her apartment house. I figured she might spot the Pontiac in which I had driven her home from Ribaldo's on that much-remembered night. In the Ford I had installed the receiver and a miniaturized tape recorder that was voice-actuated.

I waited a week, taping every incoming

and outgoing call from her apartment. There were the usual orders to meat markets, liquor stores, department stores in the city, etc. And there were a lot of calls to and from women friends. Martha Wallace sure knew a lot of gals who had nothing to do on a summer morning but gab and exchange dirty jokes. Those jokes! Too bad I could never repeat them—even at a smoker.

After a week of this, I took my library of tapes back to my motel room and played them all over again—once, twice, three times, trying to find a pattern. There was nothing I could spot—except that three times during the week she had a lunch date with some gal called Mary McCartney. I played the McCartney sections again. There was no mention of where they were to meet for lunch—just the phrase "the usual place," spoken either by Martha or the McCartney dame.

I looked up McCartney in all the local telephone directories. The only McCartney listed was a delicatessen in River Hill, and when I called one afternoon and asked for "Mary," a gruff male voice told me to get lost. His name was Mike, and there was no Mary McCartney at that number.

I was getting a little interested. Not excited, mind you, but a little stirred. Something just didn't smell right.

Back I went with my Ford and receiver and tape recorder the next week. About 10:00 A.M. Monday morning, another call came through to Martha's phone from Mary McCartney. The two woman chatted a moment, and I realized the McCartney voice sounded a little faked, a little muffled, like someone speaking in a falsetto into a glass tilted toward the phone receiver. They made a date to meet for lunch at "the usual place" at 12:00. They hung up, and a few minutes later Martha Wallace came out of her apartment and got into her imported car. Naturally I was right behind her in the Ford— well, not *right* behind her, but close enough so she'd have trouble losing me.

I guess I didn't start to get real itchy until we had driven for almost 30 minutes, and I suddenly realized it was a hell of a long way to go for lunch three or four times a week to meet a girlfriend. As a matter of fact, Martha Wallace drove for a little over an hour and was way over on the other side of the Island before she pulled into the Shady Mount Motel and coasted along to Cottage #17 before she stopped the car, got out and went into the room without bothering to knock on the door.

I parked off the highway and sat there a few minutes, figuring my move. I finally decided I'd be an idiot to call the fuzz with nothing more than a suspicion. I got out of the Ford, locked the doors and walked across to the motel office.

There was an old biddy on the desk, working at a huge, old-fashioned ledger, and she didn't even look up when I came in.

"I'm looking for Mr. Walker," I said loudly. "In Cottage 17, I think."

"We got no Walker here," she growled.

"Winston?" I tried. "Wister? Walster? Something like that. I'm very bad at remembering names."

She looked up then and inspected me. "Walash," she said. "Mr. Walash is in 17."

I should have known he'd use part of the name of his ex-housekeeper.

"That's it!" I said cheerfully. "That's the man. I'll just go down and rap on his door. He's expecting me."

She looked at me shrewdly. She must have been one year younger than God, and there wasn't anything she hadn't seen.

"You law?" she asked. "Going to be trouble?"

"I don't know."

"Try not to get blood on the floor. I got top-grade hardwood floors in them cottages, and blood's hard to get out."

What a sweet old lady.

"I'll try not to bleed inside," I assured her.

The Venetian blinds were down all the way. I listened at the door for a moment but could barely hear the murmur of voices. How am I going to explain this if it's just another "innocent" boyfriend, I wondered as I kicked the door inward and went in fast, my skit out and gripped hard.

But of course it was John Wallace, even though he had started to grow a grubby little mustache. I recognized him from the photo the cops got from Martha. They both were sitting on the bed and turned to look at me with astonishment as I came in like gangbusters, waving my barker around like a maniac.

Then we all froze. It was the nuttiest thing; none of us said a word. The silence must have lasted for a full minute. Finally John Wallace drew a deep breath and let it out in a long sigh.

"Ah well," he said, "I was afraid it

wouldn't work, dear. But don't worry; it's really not very much."

"I tried," she said, looking at me. "I really tried."

"Indeed you did, Mrs. Wallace," I nodded gravely.

"Conspiracy to defraud," he said thoughtfully. "I imagine that's the most they can make stick. After all, we didn't take any money."

She got up from the bed and stretched, shoving her arms wide and arching her spine. That great, warm, strong body poked out her dress and she posed there a moment, her mouth open in a jaw-cracking yawn, her eyes staring into mine.

I suppose I shouldn't say it, but I liked both of them; they knew how to lose: no weeping, no hysteria, no violence. All the planning of the past year, all the memorized speeches, and the careful schedules, and the discussions of alternative plans—everything down the drain.

"Well," she said, "it was fun—while it lasted."

"It lasted long enough for me," I said.

She was laughing as she went out the door ahead of us. But John Wallace looked puzzled. He didn't get the joke.

The Woman in the Lake

I had been up in Boston on a real cutey. The client was a small insurance agency that covered international air freight shipments. They had been plagued by the theft of several small packets of industrial diamonds, shipped from Antwerp, Belgium, to importers in the Boston area.

It was a real mind-blast. The packets were delivered by the Antwerp exporter directly to the airport there and signed for by the captain of the air freight jet. On this side, a messenger service picked up the packets and signed for them. If the plane arrived after 3:00 P.M., the packets were brought through customs and then put in the messenger service's vault at the airport overnight. In the morning they were taken out, placed in an armored delivery van and brought to the customer. At that time they were opened, and about one a month was found to contain gravel. Sweet . . . no?

As an agent for the International Insurance Investigators, I was handed this silly mess and told to stop it. Ordinarily our Boston office would handle it, but they figured it might be smart for a guy who had never been seen in the Boston area to come in and take a job with the messenger service delivering the diamond packets from airport to customer. So that's what we did; for three weeks I wore the coveralls of the messenger service at the airport.

Meanwhile, Gen. Lemuel K. Davidson, USMC (Ret.), boss man of the Triple-I, had our overseas office making inquiries in Antwerp. He sent me copies of their reports, and this is how it added up:

    1. Diamonds measured out from vault of exporter and wrapped. Packet given to chauffeur of exporter's own truck who signs for it.

    2. Chauffeur takes packet to airport and delivers it to air freight outfit. Representative signs for it.

    3. Representative of air freight outfit gets it through customs and delivers it to

plane. Captain of air freight jet signs for it.

4. On this side, representative of messenger outfit picks up packet from plane and signs for it.

5. If it arrives too late in the day for immediate delivery, he gets it through customs and takes it to custodian of messenger company's vault at airport. This gent signs for it and tucks it away overnight.

6. In the morning, the driver of an armored delivery van picks up the packet from the vault and signs for it. He delivers it to customer.

7. Customer opens packet, finds a lovely collection of pebbles and ashes, and says, "Omigosh," or an approximation thereof.

8. Importer calls insurance company and screams.

Our overseas branch swore the substitution was not being made on their side. They had some sharp operators working for them, and I was willing to take their word for it. That meant the switch was made on the plane or after the packet arrived in the U.S. The fact that several switches had been made on different planes, with different crews, made it extremely unlikely that a mid-air con game was taking place. And that, of course, meant that the switch took place after the gems arrived in the U.S.

So how was it done?

Like I said, I spent three weeks working for the messenger service at the Boston airport and I couldn't spot anything that wasn't copasetic. The coveralls we wore were made without any pockets whatsoever, and we dressed and undressed in a locker room scanned by closed circuit TV and constantly monitored by a security officer. Every employee went through a complete search before being allowed through the gate.

I watched everything with the Lannihan eagle eye, listened to all the gossip, suspected everyone, learned absolutely nothing . . . and during the third week I was there, a $30,000 packet of diamonds was replaced with a neat box of walnut shells.

So naturally I did the only thing any normal man would do—I got drunk. And about 5:00 A.M. the next morning I sat up in my lumpy bed in my sleazy hotel room and gasped a four-letter version of "Eureka!" My temples were pounding, my throat was lined with sandpaper, my stomach was rumbling like Vesuvius . . . and I felt great.

I figured the switch was made by the guy

who picked up the packet from the plane, took it through customs and delivered it to the messenger company's vault. He was a tall, rugged guy, a war veteran, who wore a plastic-and-aluminum prosthetic device to replace a leg he had left in the Mekong Delta. Who's going to search a false leg?

I imagined he carried a small wrapped and addressed packet in the plastic calf of that leg. It would take him maybe five seconds to make the switch while driving his three-wheeled van from plane to vault. He waited until a packet came through of about the same size and weight as the one he had concealed, addressed to the same importer. Then he made the switch.

I called General Davidson and gave him the poop. He had our labs make up several dummy packets, each containing a miniaturized radio receiver and an alarm bell. The dummy packets were air-shipped to Antwerp, then sent back to Boston at three-day intervals. We caught him on the fourth packet.

He started walking out the gate, came within range of the transmitter we had set up . . . and his leg started ringing.

So . . . back to New York I went, grinning like an idiot. It wasn't the biggest case I've ever worked on, or the most dangerous, but the fact that I cracked it while suffering from the world's most shattering hangover pleased me. There's much to be said for alcohol.

I expected a growled, "Well done," from General Davidson—his highest praise—but instead I got a half-hour lecture on my "inflated expenses" while in Boston and the "absolute necessity" for keeping agents' expenditures at a "rock-bottom minimum." Having cut down my ego to its proper dwarf level, the General then picked up a file from his desk and harrumphed a few times. This was to impress me with the seriousness of what he was about to reveal. He began reading from the file:

"CLIENT: Barthold Insurance Co. Ltd. SUBJECT: Miss Anne Cabot Gregory. INQUIRY: Life insurance policy in the sum of $150,000, double indemnity in case of accidental death. Subject deceased while engaged in underwater research in lake on St. Crispin Island. BENEFICIARIES: Shirley Gregory, a sister, and Dr. Simon Halver. Subject was engaged to Dr. Halver."

I watched a pigeon land on the General's

windowsill and start preening its wing feathers. I heard Davidson drone on and on, but I really wasn't listening. If it was an assignment I'd have to read the file anyway . . . this verbal briefing was a waste of time.

". . . so I suggest you make plans to leave at once," the General concluded, and I came awake.

"Leave, sir? For where?"

"St. Crispin Island, Lannihan. Haven't you been listening?"

"Oh yes, sir. But where, exactly, is St. Crispin Island?"

He tossed the file across the polished desk. It skidded to a neat stop, directly in front of me.

"British West Indies," he growled, and I could have kissed him. After three wet, cold weeks in Boston, this was exactly what I needed and wanted. And, of course, the old bastard knew it. This was my Tootsie Roll for breaking the diamond packet case. Somewhere in that barrel chest was a heart—small, perhaps . . . maybe even shriveled . . . but a heart nevertheless.

"Thank *you*, sir!" I said, grabbing the file and standing.

"And watch those expenses," he shouted after me. "It is extremely important that every employee recognize the importance of keeping unnecessary expenditures to an . . ."

I closed the door softly behind me.

It took me a long time to pack—maybe ten minutes. The office handled the nitty-gritty of reservations, and eight hours later I looked out the window of a British Airways jet and saw nothing below but shimmering waves. The view in the cabin was better, the stewardess had legs that dreams are made of. And in my hand was a tall noggin of bourbon and water.

"Oh, paradise . . ." I quoted.

"Did you call, sir?" Miss Legs asked.

"Marry me," I said, and she laughed.

Life *can* be beautiful.

As the jet started its descent, beginning to let down almost an hour before the scheduled landing time on St. Crispin Island, I opened the file tagged "Gregory, Anne Cabot, deceased," and began reading. The facts were few and not very revealing . . .

Dr. Anne Gregory had been a professor of marine biology at a large midwestern university. Three years ago her father had died, leaving her an inheritance sufficiently large to enable her to retire permanently to St. Crispin. She bought a home on the shore of an inland, fresh-water lake, and began a study of the ecology of the lake. A year ago she published her findings in a book entitled *A World of Microcosm*. Unexpectedly, for a work of such a technical nature, it became a popular best-seller, and Dr. Gregory was praised for her perceptive insight into the lives of the tiny marine creatures that were her specialty, as well as for her graceful prose style.

Sooo . . . here we have a world-famous woman writer and authority, living on a tiny dot of land in the middle of the Caribbean. Living with her was her younger sister, Shirley. A house guest at the time of the alleged accident that brought the brilliant career of Anne Gregory to a fast finish was Dr. Simon Halver, who had been a former colleague of Anne's at that midwestern university. There were two servants in the house, natives of St. Crispin, Timothy and Dorothy Tavish, a married couple.

Even after the publication of her book, Dr. Gregory continued her daily explorations of nearby Barnaby Lake, using a rubber diving suit and face mask with extended snorkel to explore the bottom of the lake. The lake itself was quite shallow in most places, and the bottom could easily be examined by a swimmer equipped with a snorkel rather than air tanks. Only in the center of the lake was there a relatively deep area where the bottom ran about 20 feet below the surface.

On the day of her death, Dr. Anne Cabot Gregory started out, as usual, at about 11:00 A.M. to explore the lake, wearing her rubber swimsuit and diving mask. It was a walk of barely 100 yards from her house to the shore of Barnaby Lake. She was seen adjusting her face mask and entering the water by both servants, Timothy and Dorothy Tavish. A few moments later Shirley Gregory and Dr. Simon Halver drove into the tiny town of Bay's End to buy fresh fruit and seafood for the big meal of the day, which was usually served at about 1:00 P.M.

Shirley and Dr. Halver returned from town about 12:30. They brought their purchases into the kitchen where both Timothy and Dorothy Tavish were preparing dinner. Dr. Anne Gregory had not yet returned from her underwater explorations of Barnaby Lake.

And she hadn't returned by 1:15. Shirley and Dr. Halver began to get a bit restive. They wandered down to the shore of the lake and took a look around. No Anne. By 2:00, they were really worried and enlisted the help of the Tavishes. Shirley and Dr. Halver started out around the west shore of the lake; the Tavishes took the eastern path.

The Tavishes found her. She was floating on her back in a tiny cove, arms and legs outspread. Her snorkel and face mask were missing, but there were no signs of violence. However, she was quite dead . . .

"Accidental drowning" was the verdict of St. Crispin's coroner. But Dr. Anne Gregory carried a $150,000 policy with the Barthold Insurance Co. Ltd., with a double-indemnity clause in case of accidental death that made Barthold liable for a $300,000 nick. They didn't like this. So naturally they screamed to the Triple-I for an independent investigation.

. . . And that's all I had to go on—except that Shirley Gregory would benefit to the extent of $240,000 from her sister's watery death, and Dr. Simon Halver would receive $60,000. He had been engaged to marry the deceased woman.

I took a room at a hotel called—so help me!—Pirates' Roost in the middle of the town of Bay's End. The hotel was white-washed stucco, had rooms just slightly smaller than the men's room at Radio City and used those old-fashioned, slow-turning ceiling fans to cool the joint. The bar was a dim oasis of bamboo and polished mahogany with a generous supply of every alcoholic beverage known to living man. I had a tiny balcony outside my room where I could sit in a wicker chair, gnaw on a glass of bourbon and watch the silly moon slide up out of the Caribbean.

Paradise? It would do until the real thing came along.

I woke the next morning and resisted a terrible temptation to cable my immediate resignation to General Davidson. What the hell, I could always become a beach boy and learn how to weave hats out of palm fronds.

Shortly before noon I hired one of the two taxis in town (a beautifully polished and cared-for 1953 Chrysler) and directed the native driver to the Gregory home. I had called earlier in the morning, and Shirley Gregory invited me out for dinner. Nice voice on the phone ... low, husky, with a sexy tremor.

It was a great pad the late Dr. Anne Gregory had purchased on the shores of Barnaby Lake. It was one of those big, old Victorian houses, with towers and minarets and cupolas and widows' walks and ginger-bread trim and a wide, screened verandah that ran entirely around the joint. What a bordello that would have made!

As I was paying off the cab, a young woman came out the front door and started down the steps toward me. I figured her at about 23 and stacked like a pile of goose-down pillows. I mean she was *soft* and bulging in the right places, and there wasn't a straight line on her . . . anywhere. She wore her dark hair loose and it tumbled down her back almost to her waist. Her face was smooth, plump and empty. A nice smile but not too much behind it. She was barefoot and her feet were dirty. So? With a body like that, you want clean feet?

"Miss Gregory?" I asked, giving her my No. 4 smile—the slow, ironic melting of facial muscles that usually made the younger women nicker like a mare in heat.

"Oh no, sir," she grinned. "I'm Dorothy Tavish. I work here. Miss Shirley and Dr. Halver are waiting for you inside, sir."

So Lannihan switched to his No. 6 smile, the frankly ribald grin designed for maids, waitresses and secretaries. This one worked; I caught an answering pout of her fleshy lips and a twitch of soft hips under the wild, printed shift she was wearing. Oh, Lannihan . . . you crazy lover!

The dim, cool dining room of the Gregory home smelled of lemon furniture oil, fresh shrimp broiled in butter and garlic, and a French perfume that tickled the nostrils and excited the soul. The wide mahogany table was already set, and it was obvious where the first two odors were coming from. The third was being beamed my way by the young lady who rose to her feet as I entered and came toward me, hand outstretched.

"Mr. Lannihan," she said, "I'm Shirley Gregory. Welcome to St. Crispin."

Tall . . . as slender as a high-fashion model . . . a helmet of sleek, black hair, cut short . . . about 28, I guessed . . . carefully controlled features . . . calm eyes, maybe cold . . not pretty, but something, something . . . arms and legs that looked like they had been squeezed from tubes . . . flat chest . . . a marvelous tan . . . wearing a kind of muumuu that left her neck and shoulders bare . . . delectable . . .

I pressed her cool hand briefly and muttered some fast consolation about her sister's death and apologized for my intrusion. Then I became aware of the man standing in the shadowed corner of the room and turned.

"Dr. Simon Halver," Shirley Gregory gestured, and he came forward.

For some reason I wanted to slug him instead of shaking his hand. There was something about the guy that aroused all my violent instincts. Maybe it was that ridiculous thin mustache, waxed to sharp pencil points turned upward. Maybe it was his supercilious smile or the limp paw he held out for me to squeeze. Or maybe it was the fact that he was almost a head taller than me—a real *big* guy with wide shoulders sloping down to a tight stomach and slim hips. He sure didn't look like a professor.

He had a tan, too, and a mouthful of teeth as white as the keys on a new piano. I think what bugged me most was the short-sleeved sport shirt he was wearing. The sleeves were short enough, but he had rolled them up almost to his armpits. To reveal the biceps, of course; the creep was a weightlifter. Not that all weightlifters are creeps . . . but this one was, in spades.

The food was great: broiled shrimp, and chicken fried with garlic, and rice with saffron, and a fresh salad of stuff I had never tasted before. I made a pig of myself and never mentioned business until Dorothy Tavish cleared the table. Then a guy came in with coffee and a chocolate-flavored liqueur. Shirley Gregory called him "Timothy," and immediately Sherlock Holmes Lannihan deduced he was Timothy Tavish, butler of the establishment and husband of the luscious and toothsome Dorothy.

He was a small, dark-complexioned guy,

his face a mask, expressionless. He moved smoothly and quietly. I dropped a spoon and before I could even begin to bend for it, he was there in a sleek swoop, plucked it off the floor, had a clean spoon set beside my plate and made a small bow . . . all this without a gasp or caught breath. The guy was fast and oiled . . . poetry in motion. I had a crazy thought—a brief one—about matching him against the weightlifter, Dr Halver. I'd have bet on the smaller Timothy Tavish. He was polished steel.

So, finally, we got down to the nasty business of life and death. I started by explaining that I was merely a representative of the insurance company which, quite naturally, wanted to make certain that Dr. Anne Gregory's death was, in fact, an accident. Shirley Gregory and Dr. Halver nodded understandingly.

I took them through the fatal day, almost minute by minute, and they could add nothing to what I had already read in the preliminary reports.

They had gone into Bay's End at about 11:15, driving the Jeep that was the only vehicle in the family. They returned about 12:30. When Dr. Anne hadn't appeared by 1:15, they began their search.

Both of them spoke frankly and openly. They answered every question I asked. I could detect no hesitation, no fluttered eyelids, no tightening of features . . . nothing.

Finally, almost as an afterthought, I asked Dr. Halver how long he and Dr. Anne had been engaged. He was silent a moment—and then stretched. It was such a finky thing to do that I knew the question embarrassed him. He threw his muscular arms wide and arched his back. He tried a yawn—but all he did was open his mouth wide; it didn't come off.

"About six years," he said, "if it's of any importance."

I shrugged and let it alone. It bothered me, but I wasn't about to probe that particular nerve any deeper at the moment. I turned to Shirley Gregory.

"I'd like to ask two favors of you," I said politely. "If you have a photograph of the late Dr. Gregory, I'd like to see it. Also, I'd like permission to talk to Dorothy and Timothy Tavish alone, if I may."

"Of course," she agreed readily.

The photo was a good one—an 8 × 10 glossy of Dr. Anne Gregory in her rubber diving suit. She was standing easily, leaning against one of the porch pillars, one hip out-thrust. She was a big, heavy woman, but I got the impression it was all solid beef, no fat. She had coarser features than her younger sister. Her nose was thicker, her lips thinner, her jaw more prominent, her chin massive. She was a solid, determined, almost masculine woman. Very definite. Very, very definite. It was just a feeling I got from the photo. I knew I wouldn't have liked her. I wouldn't have wanted to go to bed with her. Too much chin.

I interviewed Timothy Tavish in a corner of that wide verandah that ran around the entire house. I took him over the events of the morning Dr. Anne Gregory died. He wasn't what I'd call a blabbermouth.

"You and your wife were preparing dinner?"

"Yes."

"You were both in the kitchen at the time?"

"Yes. In and out."

"What do you mean—in and out?"

"I went to the orchard for a fresh lime. My wife, she went to the vegetable garden for several things."

"So you weren't together in the kitchen all the time until Miss Shirley and Dr. Halver returned from Bay's End?"

"That is correct."

"Did you like Dr. Anne Gregory?"

"Like?"

"Is this a good job—was it a good job, working for Dr Anne?"

"Yes. Good job."

"There were no arguments? No disagreements?"

He shrugged, and something that was a pale shadow of a smile passed over his mahogany-hued features.

"We are servants," he said. "Always, eventually, between master or mistress and servants there will be disagreements. But nothing serious."

"Of course," I nodded. "And how about Miss Shirley? Do you and your wife get along with her?"

"Yes."

"And Dr. Halver?"

For a split-second I thought I saw something—a sudden flaring-up—in his blank eyes. Then it was gone.

"Yes," he said. "Dr. Halver. Very nice man."

It was like chipping away at a marble slab with a nail file. I gave it up. Timothy Tavish left me and headed toward the back of the house. A few minutes later I saw him striding toward Barnaby Lake, a fishing pole in his hand. Something nice for supper. I wished they'd ask me to stay and I knew they wouldn't.

Shirley and Dr. Halver were planning a swim in the sea. I thanked them for their cooperation, and Shirley Gregory told me that Dorothy Tavish would drive me back to my hotel in the family Jeep. After a great dinner—dessert!

She drove like a sharecropper in a Rolls, giggling like a maniac and taking curves with increased speed and a squeal of tires. I hung on, not saying a word, and closing my eyes when we took the hairpin bends on the road that clung to the cliff overlooking the sea. She pulled up in front of the Pirates' Roost with a jerk that almost twitched every one of my hairs from its individual follicle.

"Thanks a lot," I said, "and I'll be delighted to ride with you again . . . say in about a hundred years?"

She threw back her head and laughed. Fear vanished and sex appeared; I wanted to bend forward and bite that soft, limpid throat. God, that woman was something! All stupid softness and heat and smell.

"Come in for a drink?" I asked her, not thinking, just feeling.

"Of course," she shouted in that wonderful melodic, lilting accent the natives have. "Why not? Of course a drink!"

So we went into the shadowed, deserted bar of the Pirates' Roost. The bartender was delighted to see her, and they gabbled a few moments in an English so heavily accented that I caught about one word in ten. Then Dorothy and I took a table in a dark nook and I ordered up two rum punches, and she nodded enthusiastically.

"I like you," she said finally, after she had recovered. "You very nice man."

And just to prove it, she leaned into me in that dim booth, thigh to thigh, breast to my chest, and slowly, eventually, pressed her soft, wet, hot, slack lips against mine.

I knew no one else was in the room except the bartender industriously polishing an already polished champagne glass, but I've never been one for public displays of affection. I pulled away and tried to catch my breath.

"And I like you," I assured her. "You plenty nice woman. But you've got to get back to your job. No?"

Her eyes widened.

"What for?" she said.

Listen, if you find a hundred-dollar bill on

the sidewalk, are you going to stand there and wonder, "Why am I so lucky?" So five minutes later there we were in my enormous pad, the fan turning lazily above us. Boy, was that crazy. I mean it was *nuts!* She was out of that shift of hers in nothing flat. And I mean, nothing flat.

She giggled, laughed and roared with laughter. I'd never met a woman before— and I've never met one since—that treated sex as such a great big funny marvelous wonderful comfortable *joke.*

We did everything that afternoon except hang from the revolving blades of that overhead fan and go around together. If I'd had a hammock, she'd have done it standing up . . . and heaving with laughter.

She was the color of a well-smoked meerschaum and her skin had the texture of oiled silk. Ohhh, General Davidson, God bless you! We slid all over each other like two demented polliwogs, grasping and giggling, writhing and howling, grappling and sobbing. We were in and out, over and under, on top and on bottom, standing, sitting, squatting, inventing a new kind of yoga, a philosophy for two.

Sweating we were, and panting, and sobbing, and heaving, and crying out.

"Oh my goodness," she said once.

"What about your husband?" I asked a few years later.

"Oh, him . . ." She shrugged. "Who cares?"

I have to tell you that eventually I begged for mercy and asked *her* to stop! Flesh and blood can stand just so much.

So there we were, breathing like we had just competed in the 440 high hurdles at the Olympics, and grinning at each other like idiots.

"Shirley Gregory," I gasped, "she and Dr. Halver . . . they get along okay?"

"Oh sure," she said. "They like. Very close."

"Ah," I said, "very close. How close?"

She shrugged—which isn't easy when you're lying on your back in a rumpled bed. "Friends. They go swimming together. Dr. Anne, she went diving . . . exploring. You know? Gone all morning. So Miss Shirley and Dr. Halver, they went walking and swimming and driving. You know?"

I knew. In 90 percent of these insurance cases you start with the beneficiaries and work backwards. So now we've got Shirley Gregory and Dr. Simon Halver. Interesting.

I got rid of the amoral Dorothy Tavish in

time to shower, put on fresh slacks and sport shirt, and pay a visit to the Bay's End coroner.

He looked like a living version of Sidney Greenstreet after being held captive in a smokehouse for a few months. He kept chuckling and giggling and holding his belly and laughing. Eventually I learned that Dr. Anne Gregory had drowned, her rubber swimsuit showed no signs of damage and the only suspicious circumstance was the absence of her face mask and snorkel.

I thanked him, we giggled together and I went back to the Pirates' Roost. I mixed a Jim Beam, water and some melted ice cubes. I stripped naked, lay on my bed, nibbled on my drink and thought. Very difficult, the last.

I started from the beginning. Take a heavy, masculine, strong woman who's spent many hours in underwater exploration. You really don't figure her for an accidental death, particularly since she's working with a face mask and extended snorkel. It's a simple apparatus—really just a long breathing tube that pokes up above the surface with a primitive ball valve that prevents water from coming back into the tube.

If she had been wearing a closed mask,

regulator and tanks of air, that would have been an equine of a different hue.

So suddenly she's found dead, drowned, floating on the surface. I refused to buy it. There was no evidence of sudden seizure, cramps or heart attack. As they used to say in those lovely, antiquated English detective novels, "Someone had done her in."

Who? Well, her younger sister benefited by 240 grand from her death for starters. And Dr. Halver stood to gain 60 grand. I've known cases in which people were knocked off for 20 bucks. So 300 grand seemed plenty motive to me.

The late Dr. Anne Gregory was engaged to Dr. Halver. And that sexy sister, Shirley, was on the scene. So Halver digs Shirley, they both pretend to go into Bay's End on a shopping trip. But they stop a few minutes after they're out of sight of the servants. They go down to Barnaby Lake. They knock off Dr. Anne, somehow, and leave her floating, lifeless, while they continue on into Bay's End to buy their shrimp and imported garlic.

It all added up—and I didn't believe a word of it. Don't ask me why. It wasn't anything I deduced, it wasn't anything I knew that you don't know. It was just the reaction I had to the people involved.

First of all, that sister Shirley was sexy . . . but cool. I just couldn't see her inspiring any man to an act of homicide. And then there was Dr. Simon Halver, the weightlifter. You'd be surprised at how many women are uninspired by muscles. The two of them might have gone swimming together, as Dorothy Tavish said. They might have walked together and talked together and, for all I know, bedded together.

But I just didn't feel there was a great, passionate love thing going there. I just didn't *feel* it. And that, I must admit, is why I'm the second highest paid agent of the Triple-I; I don't think through my cases; I *feel* my way through them.

Well, assuming Dr. Anne didn't die a natural or accidental death, what does that leave? Nothing. Well . . . not quite nothing. It left Dorothy and Timothy Tavish, the faithful family retainers.

Up you go, idiot Lannihan, and into your clothes again. And then over to the office of Erik Barlow, Esq., a local attorney who handled legal and financial affairs for the late Dr. Anne Gregory. And there, after an hour of nasty prying, I discovered that the witnessed will of Dr. Gregory included grants of $3,000 each to Dorothy and Timothy Tavish. Not much, is it, when you rack it up against that $300,000 insurance? Still, on St. Crispin . . .

Back to that dim, deserted, glorious bar at the Pirates' Roost. Back to one, two, three Jim Beams diluted somewhat with soda this time. Plenty of heavy thought. Motive? Time? Method? Ability?

Later, when I went back over it in my own mind, it seemed to me the key to the whole thing was that photo of Dr. Anne Gregory I had seen—the big, coarse, beefy woman. That photo plus the fact that she had been engaged to Dr. Simon Halver for six years and they had never married. Long engagement.

That crazy moon was sneaking up out of the Caribbean again before I got out of my wicker chair on the balcony and called the Gregory house. Luckily I got Dorothy Tavish, and after a few minutes of giggling she agreed to meet me on the beach in half an hour—a stretch of sand about three minutes' walk from the Gregory home.

I went downstairs and woke up my cab driver. A double sawbuck hired the cab for the remainder of the night. He went home and I drove toward the sea. I parked a few hundred yards from the house and walked on down to the sand. She was there, waiting for me.

It was like we were starting all over again, new people, and we had never had that crazy afternoon together at the Pirates' Roost. She was primed and ready. I was ready but not quite primed.

She was as nutty as ever, laughing and squirming and all over me like a wet sheet.

"Listen," I said, "I've been talking to Miss Shirley. You know, I think she's been repressed. I think she'd like to cut loose."

"Oh yes." Dorothy Tavish giggled. "Miss Shirley, she never does nothing. She should do something."

"You bet," I agreed enthusiastically. "What would you think about you and me and Miss Shirley making a scene together? You know—the whole bit. You and her and me. Fun . . . no?"

She howled with laughter.

"Yes, yes, yes," she spluttered. "Sure. Why not. Very funny. We have fun."

"And did you have fun with Dr. Anne before she died?"

I could almost hear her tiny, tiny mind ticking over.

"Oh sure," she said finally, slowly. "We had fun."

I left her there. I mean I turned around and walked away from her, leaving her lying on the warm sand watching clouds shining in the glow of the moon like oil on water. I walked directly back to the Gregory house. I walked through the front door. I walked through the living room where Shirley Gregory and Dr. Halver were seated on separate chairs reading their separate books. They looked up at me like I was some kind of a nut they had never seen before. I guess I looked like one.

I stalked right back to the kitchen. Timothy Tavish was seated at the table, peeling some kind of fruit. He looked up slowly when I came in.

"Strong," I said, looking at him closely. "Probably a helluva swimmer. Been around water all your life. A deep diver without breathing gear."

"Sir?" he said.

"So you found out what was going on between Dr. Anne and your wife. It didn't mean a thing to her. Nothing does. But it meant a lot to you. And maybe, somehow, you found out about that kiss she left you in her will. Three grand for you and three for your wife. You can live on that a long time on St. Crispin."

"Sir?" he said.

"So your wife was in the kitchen while Dr. Anne was swimming around out there with her snorkel. And you left the kitchen to pick limes or gather rosebuds or whatever the hell you told her you were going to do. She wouldn't care, or even understand. A beautiful, warm woman—but stupid."

"Ah," he said.

"How did you do it?" I asked him. "Slash the snorkel and mask? Probably not. It might have cut her, and the coroner said she had no cuts. I'd guess you went down into the deep in the center of the lake and then came up under her. Wrenched off the face mask, grabbed her around the legs and pulled her down. She was a strong woman, but you're no weakling. Did she thresh around? Did she fight you?"

My God, was he fast! He didn't come around the table, he came over it, in one long, smooth leap, right for my throat. Before I knew it, I was flat on the floor, two hands around my throat and crazy lights already flickering behind my eyelids.

I got a knee into his groin and he moaned once and rolled away. I tried to get to my feet but he was, as I said, oiled steel. I couldn't slow him. He was all over me. He was using flat palms and bent knuckles, hitting me where it hurt, and I knew I couldn't take much more of it. I tried to set him up for something . . . anything . . . but he was too fast. He slipped everything I threw at him, and he was in front of me, below . . . I didn't know where the hell he was.

I got in one good kick but he turned to take it on his hip. Still, it staggered him long enough for me to pick up a chair. When he came in again I made toothpicks out of it on his head and shoulders, and it didn't stop him. Then I was conscious of Dr. Halver coming through the door. Tavish didn't even see him; he was crouched, his arms outspread, and he was coming for me hissing, a funny dribbling sound coming out of his open mouth.

Thank God for weightlifters. Halver clenched his two hands together, raised them in the air like a club and brought them down on the back of Timothy's neck, just where it joins the skull. There was a very satisfying crunch.

"So what else is new?" I gasped.

It took three days to wrap everything up to the satisfaction of the law enforcement officials of St. Crispin. Shirley Gregory and Dr. Halver seemed to be spending most of their off-moments together. Meanwhile, I tried to explain to Dorothy Tavish what had happened. I explained and explained, and she giggled and giggled. Her husband would probably go into durance vile for the rest of his life, but it was all a big, fat joke to her.

Meanwhile, there were men, women, boys, girls, snakes, cocker spaniels, doorknobs, knitting needles, donkeys and potato mashers. She didn't care. She giggled.

And as the sun slowly sank over the ocean, I departed the glorious shores of St. Crispin, land of the loonies. It was a great vacation while it lasted—and if it had lasted much longer they would have taken me home on a stretcher. It wasn't the damage Timothy Tavish had done to me; it was what his wife did.

A String of Blues

Way back in 1798, a cat named Frederico, Duke of Luchesa, was caught cheating on his mistress; Freddy spent the night with his wife. To smooth things over, the Duke ordered up a bauble for his 15-year-old girlfriend. It was a necklace of 20 marquise-cut 10-carat blue diamonds. It was designed and put together by Ignace Schifarri of Milan. Apparently it did the trick; the Duke of Luchesa finally died at the age of 92 from exhaustion. Is there a better way to go? The necklace got the name of the "Schifarri String" and it passed through the hands of several owners over the years and the centuries. Originally, the string supported a 24-carat pendant, but during World War I, the owner (the English Lady Cynthia Cummings) found it necessary to sell off the large stone. The necklace was then redesigned as a rather loose choker by Charles of London. To tell you the truth, it was not a first-class string: the third stone to the right of the clasp and the fifth stone to the left had slight imperfections. Still, the Schifarri String was a lovely collection of blue diamonds in elegant settings, and the last time the string was sold, the price was just under $500,000.

The ice came to this country in 1893, purchased at an Amsterdam auction by Horace J. Mandible, a Chicago meat packer. When they nabbed Horace on a fraud case (he wasn't packing *quite* as many hams as he told his stockholders), the Schifarri String went on the open market. It was bought by Eugene Snipes III. His son gave it to his bride—the former Evelyn Burroughs of Grosse Point—as a wedding present. I often thought this was strictly cheapsville on the part of Eugene Snipes IV, since the ice was in the family and didn't cost him a cent. Mr. and Mrs. Eugene Snipes IV got a Las Vegas divorce about two years ago. Under the terms of the settlement, the Schifarri String remained in the possession of Evelyn Snipes. On April 13, it was stolen from her townhouse on East 73rd Street, New York City.

And that's how I got to know all these mind-blowing facts about the Schifarri String. The necklace was insured by Revere & Sons,

Boston—a very old, very conservative, very staid company with a one-man Claims Department. When it appeared that they might have to take a $500,000 nick, old man Paul Revere (so help me, that was his name) decided to take advantage of the retainer he had been paying the International Insurance Investigators, Inc., for lo, these many years.

Boss man of the Triple-I was General Lemuel K. Davidson, USMC (Ret.). He dumped the Snipes file in my lap, muttered some nonsense about "quick results" and turned me loose. As usual, my job as claims investigator was to turn up evidence of possible fraud or to pass the sad word along to Revere & Sons to pony up the 500 G's. Or to make a deal with the crooks and recover the Schifarri String for much less than 500 G's—if Revere & Sons would stand still for such a shady deal. After reading up on the history of the diamonds—which I have condensed above out of consideration for your boredom level—I went to visit the divorced Evelyn Burroughs. The fact that she had re-adopted her maiden name led me to believe that the divorce from Eugene Snipes IV was not one of those partings in which the once wed remain "absolutely the best of friends, my dear." Evelyn was, I guessed, on the far side of 35. She was a stringbean of a woman, tall and slender, with no noticeable curves. But the skin of her face, chin and throat was smooth and unwrinkled, and she moved with a kind of lanky grace that spelled plenty of physical exercise, good muscle tone and probably two or three massages a week.

She could afford them; that was for sure. Her townhouse, in one of the most expensive neighborhoods in Manhattan, was four stories of grey stone, with a copper roof and round stained-glass windows set over the ornate doorway. She received me (after I was announced by a uniformed maid) in a wood-paneled study that didn't have quite as many books as the Library of Congress . . . but almost.

Her voice was level, low-pitched, almost without a discernible accent or dialect. She spoke steadily and without faltering, and never let her eyes waver from mine. Since she talked for almost five minutes, that was quite a trick. Try looking someone else directly in the eyes for five minutes; it's practically impossible.

Her story was simple enough. It was the maid's day off on the date the theft occurred. Evelyn had gone shopping. When she returned, the front door was closed but unlocked. She remembered very well locking it before she left. She knew almost immediately that someone had been or was still in the house, several things had been moved out of position: books pulled from shelves, pictures shifted on the walls, etc. Thereupon Evelyn did something very smart: she left her home, went to the apartment house next door and called the cops.

They searched the place. More disarray on the upper floors. They asked Miss Burroughs to take a quick inventory, which she did. The only thing missing was the Schifarri String.

I asked her if she had worn the necklace to any private or public gatherings or parties recently. She said she had; she *always* wore the string when she went out in the evening; it was her favorite. No, she had noticed nothing suspicious; no one asked her questions about it; no one followed her home as far as she knew; her home had never been robbed before.

She sat in a straight-backed chair, leaning forward slightly as she spoke. Her ankles were crossed modestly and her hands were folded gracefully in her lap. She was the coldest, calmest, most self-contained woman I had ever met. Never once did she hesitate over a word. Never once did her voice falter. Never once did she twitch or squirm in the chair or poke a finger into her hair or examine her nails or do any of the hundreds of other things people normally do when they're speaking. It was a hell of a performance, and I looked at her more closely.

Straight spine . . . erect posture . . . wide shoulders . . . a strong neck . . . a dark, spade-shaped face made up to accent high cheekbones and slightly slanted eyes. A thin nose . . . small ears flat to her skull . . . dark, glossy hair cut quite short. As I said, slender and willowy . . . tiny waist . . . thin hips and a hard rump (no girdle-wearer she) . . . and really magnificent legs, incredible legs, with calves a bit larger than knees and great curves all the way. Good feet, too, and apparently she was vain about them: the shoes were paper-thin soles, a couple of patent-leather straps and not much else. Those sexy, sensuous legs and feet just didn't go with the rest of her body.

When she finished her story, I nodded sympathetically and assured her my investigation was purely routine. I asked if I might speak to the maid for a few minutes.

"Of course," she said, rising to her feet in

a flowing movement that was pure poetry, "I'll send her."

She had the tact not to be present when I interviewed the maid, which was fine with me. The maid was a cute little butterball, a Swedish girl who had been in the U.S. less than a year. She said "Yah" to practically every question I asked, and did a great deal of high-pitched giggling. I knew, from a report in the file General Davidson had given me, that the cops had given Ilse Swensen a clearance—temporarily. After talking to her, I thought the cops were right. Ilse pulling a gem theft was like Bozo the Clown inventing the atom bomb.

"I suppose Miss Burroughs goes out a lot?" I said finally, snapping shut my little notebook. (This is a calculated maneuver; it makes the witness think you've stopped taking notes and everything else said is off the record.)

"Oh, yah!" Ilse giggled.

"Anyone special?"

"Special?"

"Any one man she sees a lot of? A man who's been here several times or calls for her?"

"Nooo . . . no one, Mostly with couples she goes out. Friends. Sometimes men have picked her up or come for dinner. But always different men."

"Do you think she's a happy woman, Ilse?"

"Happy? Oh, yah! Miss Burroughs very happy. Very nice lady. Sings all the time. Laughs."

"She does, eh? And she's always been like this—ever since you've worked for her?"

"Oh no. At first, the lady was very dark, gloomy. She sat alone in here, read books. You know? But that was right after her divorce."

"She was divorced two years ago. You've been with her less than a year."

"Yah? That's right."

"But when you first came here she was dark and gloomy? Then she began to get happy?"

"Yah."

"When did she start to get happy? When did she start to sing?"

"Oh, maybe six months ago."

"Thank you, Ilse. You've been very helpful and you're a very pretty young woman."

"Oh, yah!"

I went over to see Detective-Two Barney Wyatt who was handling the sheet on the case. I took him out to a nearby saloon and we had a few Jim Beams.

"Good sippin' whiskey," Barney nodded approvingly. "What have you got?"

I told him the results of my interviews, and Barney listened closely.

"Forget about the maid," he advised me after I'd finished. "We checked her out thoroughly . . . even put a tail on her for a week. I think she's clean. Incidentally, if you're interested, on her day off she goes to a pool and sauna up in Yorkville. How would you like to see that in a bikini?"

"Barney," I said, "have another drink. You don't have to be old to be a dirty old man."

We went over the puzzling aspects of the case. (1) Books were pulled from shelves and pictures tilted on walls, but nothing had been cut or ripped—standard operating procedures when a hood in a hurry is looking for jewels or cash. (2) The front door had been unlocked with not even a hint of forcible entry—and the lock was a good one with a top-to-bottom steel flange that overlapped the frame, meaning the celluloid strip technique couldn't have been used. (3) Nothing had been taken but the Schifarri String, although other jewels were in a case in the bedroom closet and even lying on the dresser.

"It could be a special-order job," I suggested to Wyatt. "A crook jeweler gets an order, probably from overseas, for a string of matched 10-carat blues. He knows the Schifarri String, just like he knows every other expensive gem in the world. So he calls in a pro to lift this particular string and nothing else."

Barney shook his head. "Won't wash. This campaign screams 'amateur.' I swear it wasn't a pro. Besides, I don't think the rocks are out of the country—and you don't either."

"No," I confessed, "I don't."

"So you're going to call every fence and nark in town, putting out the word that you're ready to deal?"

"I've got to, Barney. That's my job."

"Yeah," he said disgustedly, "that's your job."

"One other thing I'm going to do, Barney. I'm going to start living with Evelyn Burroughs."

"Lots of luck," he nodded. "Keep me informed."

I took up station at 9:00 A.M. the next morning, parking about halfway down the block from her townhouse. She came out about 10:00, walked a block, took a cab and headed downtown, with me a few cars behind. The hack dropped her at Libby & Sons—possibly New York's swankiest department store. I parked in a bus loading zone, figure the Triple-I would square the ticket.

Libby & Sons is never that crowded that you get lost in the mob. I picked her up at the perfume counter, staying well out of sight behind a pillar. She didn't show any signs of suspecting a tail, but this dame was so cool and self-possessed that it was hard to tell what she was thinking.

She took the escalator to the second floor: Ladies Shoes. I went up right behind her, turned in the opposite direction and strolled around Fun Shoes for the Beach. No one bothered me; in Libby's you pleaded with a salesclerk to help you; they don't brace you.

I saw her walk into the main shoe department. A man came forward, smiled, bowed, and shook her proffered hand. He was about 55, white-haired, with an up-curled handlebar mustache I envied. She sat down and he started bringing out boxes of shoes. She tried them all on, and they laughed and chatted for almost 30 minutes before she departed without buying anything.

A stroll up Madison Avenue, looking in shop windows. Luncheon with a girlfriend she met at L'Auglone's. More window shopping. I was getting hungry. The two women separated at the corner of 43rd and Fifth, pecking each other on the cheek.

Evelyn Burroughs walked across to First Avenue and took an uptown bus. I followed in a cab. She got back to her home about 4:15. I thought she was safe for awhile and went back downtown to reclaim my four-year-old Pontiac from the bus loading zone. I figured I'd have at least one ticket. I didn't. The car had been towed away.

And what a lovely zero day it had been!

I spent eight more days at this nonsense, never feeling sure enough of my suspicions to ask headquarters for a relief. It wouldn't have done any good anyway, as far as I could see. She went shopping almost every morning. She went to a matinee on Wednesday afternoon. She met various girlfriends (never a man) and lunched at expensive joints. In the evenings she stayed home most of the time. Occasionally she had a date—either sashaying out by herself to a charity affair or being called for by a couple.

I was wasting a lot of the Triple-I's time and money, and I was getting awfully sick of nibbling on bologna sandwiches while she was in some fancy dive teething on a frog's leg sautéed in butter and garlic.

After more than a week of this, I gave up after she turned once more into Libby & Sons. I went back to my pad, kicked off my shoes, slit open a new jar of Jim Beam and gulped down a rich highball before I even allowed myself to think.

As Barney Wyatt knew I would, I had sent the word out to every fence and rock man in town: Wanted—the Schifarri String: 100 G's paid immediately; no questions asked.

Not a nibble.

I went over the voluminous notes I had made during my week of tailing Miss B. I read them through, then once again, then once again. I was trying to spot some kind of a pattern, or something that didn't fit into the expected routine of a rich bitch with plenty of time and money to spend.

I was on my third Beam—frantic enough now to be sloshing it onto the rocks—when something caught my eye. I went back over my notes once again, There it was:

Tuesday; 10:43; Libby & Sons; shoe dep't; no purchase.

Thursday; 11:42; Libby & Sons; shoe dep't; no purchase.

Monday; 11:09; Libby & Sons; shoe dep't; no purchase.

I know that dames like to try on shoes, especially when they think they've got feet that should be cast in bronze, but three visits to the same store, the same shoe department in one week, with no purchases made?

I got on the horn to Wyatt.

"Barney," I said, "do me a favor?"

"Depends."

"It's the Schifarri String. Might be something good for you."

"Let's have it."

"There's a clerk in the shoe department of Libby & Sons. Male, white, about 55, about 5-8, about 185. Sharp dresser. Florid complexion. White hair. White handlebar mustache. Can't miss him."

"So?"

"Can you get me a make?"

There was silence for a moment.

"Shouldn't be hard," Barney said finally. "They've got a good security system. Guy who runs it used to be one of ours—Eddie Price. He lost an arm in a crackup when he was chasing a bank man. I'll get hold of him. Take about a day or so."

"Thanks, Barney. It might be nothing. It might be something."

The next day Mr. Paul Revere, of Revere & Sons, Boston, received a typewritten letter, unsigned, postmarked New York City. It stated that the writer was in possession of the Schifarri String and would be willing to relinquish it to Revere & Sons upon the payment of $250,000 which, the writer was thoughtful enough to point out, would save the insurance company from paying out 500 G's for total loss.

The letter suggested that, if Revere & Sons was interested in this arrangement, a suitable personal ad be inserted in the morning edition of the *New York Globe* on Wednesday next, stating that further details were requested in the "Schifarri Affair."

Mr. Paul Revere called Gen. Lemuel Davidson. The General called me. I told them to insert the ad. Meanwhile, the letter was brought down to New York by an air messenger and put through the mill at the Triple-I labs. It took them less than an hour to determine that the paper was a cheap variety, without rag content, available in thousands of stationery and notion stores. The typewriter used was a 1974 Remington portable. The person who typed it was probably left-handed, had a heavy touch and appeared to be a man of some education.

The ad was placed, and two days later I was sitting in my broom-closet office in the Triple-I headquarters, trying to get caught up on my paper work, when the phone rang.

"Lannihan."

"Barney Wyatt here. Wolf, you know that shoe salesman in Libby & Sons you asked about?"

"Yeah?"

"Name's Timothy Neill, 54, native of Ireland. Been employed there for two years. Lives in a hotel on the West Side—76th Street. Single."

"Well . . . I guess that's it. Sorry it went sour, Barney, but thanks for your help."

"Oh, one more thing. You sounded so interested that I had Eddie Rice send over a patent-leather shoe this guy handled. We pulled his prints and sent them down to Washington. He's really Thomas Natalie, a con man with a sheet as long as your arm. Mostly conspiracy to commit fraud, but also some rough stuff in his younger days. Warrants in three states and Canada."

"You son of a bitch," I yelled. "Why couldn't you have told me that first?"

"I wanted to make you happy," he said. "Want us to take it from here?"

"Not yet," I said. "It's just beginning to heat up. We've got nothing to take to court at the moment. But I'll keep you in the picture."

Then I told him about the letter Revere & Sons had received, and in return he gave me Natalie's hotel address.

I went to Libby & Sons first to make certain Natalie was there, slipping under-sized pumps onto the swollen feet of fat dowagers. (Sure I'm cautious; that's why I'm alive.) Then I drove up to Natalie's hotel.

It was a fleabag, painted in a color they used to call "shocking pink," and from out-side the whole place looked like it had been condemned by the Board of Health and no one had bothered to tell the occupants. From the doorway I had a good view of the desk, and I lolled about a few minutes until the clerk stepped into the back office. Then I walked quickly across the small lobby and ran up the grease-encrusted stairway. It was that easy.

Natalie's room was 2-B. The door was locked, but I could get 20 years for what I know about opening locked doors. This one took me about three seconds with the aid of a plastic credit card and a hard slam just above the lock.

The first thing I saw, sitting on a ramshackle table, was a Remington portable typewriter. I felt great. It was a feeling that gradually disappeared during the next hour as I took the place apart—carefully and neatly—and found nothing. I checked the old-fashioned chandelier and toilet tank, felt over the iron-firm mattress carefully, turned dresser and closet inside out. Nothing.

So maybe it was a bad guess. I went over ventilators, wall plates and radiators. Still nothing. I was steaming from my hurried exertions and walked over to the single paint-encrusted window, figuring to let a little air into the place. And there it was.

A thin, transparent nylon cord coming into the room under the window sash. And there, on the outside sill, a small leather bag en-cased in a clear plastic bag.

"Hello there," I said happily.

I hauled it in carefully, opened both bags and spilled the gems into my palm. Jesus, they were beautiful. Even in the lousy hotel room lighting they winked and twinkled and glowed with a life all their own. I could understand why men and women were willing to steal and kill to get them. The damn things were sexual: alive and throbbing.

I thought a long while, then carefully replaced the Schifarri String in the two bags and hung them outside exactly where they had been before. I straightened up the rooms, and left the door properly locked behind me. The room clerk didn't even glance at me when I walked out. It was that kind of hotel.

The ad in the *Globe* brought quick results. Paul Revere up in Boston received a Special Delivery letter from New York—same paper, same typewriter—setting up a meet in an East Side tavern about a week away. That was fine for what I had in mind.

I talked General Davidson into advancing me $1,500 that could be charged against the client. I had Revere & Sons send down a complete description and photos of the Schifarri String. I had a glass duplicate made by a guy we use for this kind of work. He also works for the Other Side—but that's neither here nor there. The guy's a great craftsman, and he delivered to me a string of what, to my inexperienced eye, looked exactly like the matched 10-carat blues. Beautiful.

So, now to action . . . I went back to Natalie's room in the hotel on 76th Street, after checking once again that he was at work at Libby & Sons. I hauled in the real Schifarri String, pocketed them and replaced them with the glass duplicates. Then I went to Barney Wyatt and Confessed All.

He cursed and called me all kinds of dirty names and then laughed some, and we set it up. We waited for the maid's day off, waited until Evelyn Burroughs had left the house on her daily shopping tour, then we went in and bugged the joint from attic to basement. Illegal? I suppose so. But who's to sue? I had a feeling those tapes would never be produced in court.

The meet with the guy who had written the letters to Revere was set up for 7:00 P.M. on a Wednesday evening. I was there right on the dot but nothing happened and no one approached me. I wasn't worried; that's how these things are handled. I could see Thomas Natalie from where I was sitting. He was standing at the bar, a pint of suds in his fist, and even from my back table I could see how his head was swiveling as he checked to make certain I wasn't accompanied by a platoon of fuzz ready to swoop the moment he made contact.

He licked the foam off his mustache and departed. I sat quietly at my back table (as his second letter had requested) and waited. Sure enough, in ten minutes the bartender wandered over and delivered a note he said a "gentleman" at the bar had asked him to give me. The note suggested I try a certain bar on West 72nd Street, in a French restaurant.

So about half an hour later there I was, on the West Side this time. I was on my second Jim Beam when in strolls Thomas Natalie, better known to the shoe customers of Libby & Sons as Timothy Neill. He plunked himself down opposite me and smiled, revealing as bright a set of dentures as ever I've seen.

"You've got the lolly?" he asked.

"Of course I don't have the lolly," I said in an insulted tone. "Do you think I walk around with 250 big ones—just in case you have a few boys outside and might want the cash as well as the stones? What do you take me for?"

"Ah," he said, "a hard one."

"Exactly," I said. "I'm just here to make certain you've got what you claim you have. You'd be surprised by the number of kooks and nuts who have contacted us, claiming they have the real and original Schifarri String."

"Shocking," he said.

143

"You can say that again," I nodded. "All right, let's see what you've got."

He looked around carefully, hunched over the table, took the leather pouch out of his inside jacket pocket. He spilled the gems onto his palm and held them out to me.

"The real thing," he breathed.

I stared at them. I poked them with a finger. Then I sighed deeply, got up and pulled on my trenchcoat.

"Nice try," I said, "but no cigar. A lovely glass production. Worth maybe a grand."

I looked down at him as his face fell apart. The jaw sagged, bags suddenly appeared under the eyes, the brave mustache drooped and he aged 20 years: while I watched.

"Wha—wha—wha—," he burbled.

"Go ahead," I said, "try to scratch a window with the stones. What do you think— we were born yesterday? So long, mooch."

I turned and walked out steadily. I was parked around the corner, and from now, everything depended on timing. We were cutting it awfully close.

Mr. Paul Revere, Barney Wyatt and a cat from the DA's office were waiting for me a few doors down from Evelyn Burroughs' home. Revere had set up an appointment with the lady for 8:30 that evening. The moment I pulled up, they got out of their car and the four of us marched up to the door. It was only about 8:40. The giggling maid let us in immediately.

I had warned them to make it as fast as they could, and Revere wasted no time.

"Miss Burroughs," he said in his toneless New England twang, "I am indeed happy to be the bearer of good tidings. Through the fine efforts of these gentlemen, we have succeeded in recovering the Schifarri String, and I take great pleasure in returning it to you in the presence of these gentlemen and witnesses. Will you inspect it, please."

He handed over a deep blue velvet box in which the real Schifarri String had lovingly been laid to rest, and it was her turn to go, "Wha—wha—wha—"

After she agreed it was her necklace, in the presence of all us gentlemen and witnesses, Revere carried on his lock-jawed, school-masterish style:

"As you know, Miss Burroughs, your policy with Revere & Sons can be cancelled at will at the desire of either party concerned. We are, therefore, cancelling your policy as of this date. Here is your official notification"—he handed over an envelope—"presented to you in view of these gentlemen and witnesses who have read the contents. Good night, madam."

She was still going, "Wha—wha—wha—" when we scurried out and got into Wyatt's car down the block. The bugs in the house were connected to a central transmitter, about the size of a thimble, and Wyatt had had his engineers hook up a loudspeaker as well as a tape recorder to the transmissions.

As it turned out, we needn't have rushed; he didn't show up for another 30 minutes. Then Thomas Natalie came practically running down the street, his mouth open, gulping for air. He turned into the Burroughs home—and from then on we heard everything, and got good tapes of it, too.

The maid showed him directly to the study.

Natalie: "Glass. The goddamned thing is glass. They won't pay a cent. It's a fraud. It's nothing."

Burroughs: "What the hell are you talking about? They just returned the necklace to me. It's real. I know it's real. What's going on? What's going on?"

Natalie: "You fooled me. You fooled me. Why did you do it? Why? We could have split 250,000. I don't understand."

Burroughs: "Will you, for chrissakes, stop

gibbering? They screwed us. I've got the real necklace. Here it is. They planted an imitation on you, you old, doddering, incompetent fool."

Natalie: "Evelyn, don't talk like that, After all we've been to each other. After all—"

Burroughs: "Oh, shut your hairy mouth."

And on and on and on. I guess it would have been funny except that it was kind of tragic in a way—an old gaffer and a young (relatively) chick. A quick scheme to get some fast dough. And if you wonder why a rich bitch tried it, remember that when it comes to money, you never have enough.

I left it all in Wyatt's hands. He braced them with the tapes, and Natalie broke first—as I knew he would. He spilled everything. It had never been a love affair with them; just a "working arrangement." They never saw each other outside of those brief meetings in the shoe department of Libby & Sons. She had provided him with a key to the outside door. He had "messed things up a bit," but the Schifarri String had been the only target, and she had told him she'd leave it for him on the top of her dresser.

They both copped guilty pleas, and those disgustingly illegal tapes never were played in court. Because of his past record, he drew three-to-five. She got two, which means she'll probably be out in a few months.

Meanwhile, to finance her legal defense, the Schifarri String was put on the market. A guy named Sam Prudhahl bought it. He's a wholesale butcher from Akron. I wish him luck.

The Case of the Purloined Princess

The long-haired blonde in the itsy-bitsy, teeny-weeny pink bikini tossed back her tresses and began the long climb up the stainless steel ladder to the high board. I groaned. I watched the strong muscles of calf and thigh flex as she took each rung, watched the sun glint off her tanned, wet shoulders. I moaned.

She reached the top platform, paused a moment and took a deep breath. I whinnied. She walked out steadily to the end of the board and hooked her toes over the edge. She raised her hands high above her head and locked her thumbs. I muttered, growled and cursed.

Then she was off in a flash of tan skin and pink bikini. She entered the water as smoothly as a seal, came to the surface, shook her head once or twice and took two powerful strokes to the side of the pool. A guy who could have been a linebacker for the Packers stretched out a hand to help her out. I hated him on sight.

They went back to their table under the striped umbrella, laughing and chattering. Idiots. What could she possibly see in a guy with a full beard on his chest *and* his shoulders? I ordered up another Jim Beam-and-soda and forgot her—for all of four seconds. I closed my eyes and let my thin, city-paled skin get another dose of second-degree burns. The sky was clear, the sun was hot, the women were delightful (even if they belonged to Smokey the Bear), and I didn't care if I never saw Manhattan again.

I was in a motel in Fort Lauderdale, Florida. It was on Belmar Street, near Commercial Boulevard, and if it was any closer to the Atlantic Ocean, would be a few feet underwater. What was I doing lying at poolside, soaking up the sun's beams and liquid Beams, and dreaming of bikini-clad blondes? I was working—that's what I was doing.

It had begun about two weeks earlier. I was in my broom-closet office at headquarters of the International Insurance Investigators, making out my weekly swindle sheet and wondering if I could list the cost of cocktails for a certain young creampuff under the heading "In pursuit of wickedness."

My intercom clicked on and I heard the raspy voice of Lt. Gen. Lemuel K. Davidson, USMC (Ret.).

"Lannihan," he said, "could you stop up here a moment, please?"

He said, "please." That meant the boss had someone in the office with him. Usually he just says, "Lannihan? Now!" Like he was ordering a division to storm Mount Everest.

"Right away, sir," I answered. I straightened my tie, pulled on my jacket and headed up for the executive aerie.

Just as I figured, there was a short little runt seated in front of the General's desk. He almost got out of his chair to shake hands with me—but not quite. I got a quick impression of a face cut out of burled walnut with a dull chisel. I mean it was all lines, deep wrinkles, flat planes and strange bumps. And it was mean. Definitely not a man I'd care to spend a Saturday night with, playing pinochle and telling what happened after the farmer said, "I'm sorry; I've only got one extra bedroom, and my daughter sleeps in there."

"Lannihan," the General growled, "this

gentleman is Cyrus Vantil, head of the Claims Department of the Barnes Marine Casualty Company."

I looked at the little guy with new respect.

You've got to know that the Triple-I does claims investigation work for a flock of insurance companies and associations. We get called in when the company's own Claims Department is overworked or understaffed. Or maybe the case spreads over more than one country (the Triple-I has offices all over the world). Or maybe there's some reason why the company doesn't want its own men doing the dirty work.

Over the years I've learned that most insurance claims men would give their mothers a nickel to go to the candy store for two cents' worth of licorice—and demand three cents change when she returned. These guys are *hard*. Their job is to keep their company from being defrauded, cheated or bilked out of paying one penny more than the law requires. I mean they don't trust *anyone*. Every claim is a challenge to them, and I never met one who didn't start from the premise that there's hanky-panky going on, no matter how honest and above-board the claim might sound.

Every time I think of claims men I remember that story about two old Supreme Court justices who were riding by a meadow.

"Look at that flock of sheep over there," one of them said. "They've just been sheared."

The other judge looked and said, "They appear to have been sheared on this side."

That's the philosophy of claims men: If they can't see it, they don't believe it.

The Barnes Marine Casualty Company is one of the Triple-I's largest clients, so when General Davidson suggested I listen to the story Cyrus Vantil had to tell, I hitched my chair closer to the claims man and perked up my ears like a spooked bunny.

Actually, it turned out to be an interesting story. About 75 percent of Barnes' business, Vantil said, was insuring privately owned pleasure craft. Anything from a 10-foot rowboat to an ocean-going yacht; you name it. Fire, theft, personal liability, storm damage, loss at sea: they'd insure it . . . if you could stand the premiums.

About two years ago they began to get a lot of claims on boats apparently stolen from marinas and shipyards in the Long Island Sound area. None of the boats was ever recovered, and Barnes had to pay off. Within the past year the number of boats that disappeared almost tripled the figure their computers told them they should expect in this area.

"We assigned several men," Vantil said in a wispy, hard-to-understand voice. "They couldn't come up with anything. Finally I gave the job to our top man, Smitty Mackilson."

"Mackilson?" I interrupted. "Smith Mackilson? I think I know the guy. I worked with him on a shipyard arson case in Detroit. Tall, skinny, with an Adam's apple that bobbed up and down when he talked. Is that the guy?"

"That *was* the guy," the claims man said, without changing expression. "His body was pulled out of a drainage ditch near Fort Lauderdale, Florida, last night. That Adam's apple was sauce. He had been beaten to death with the usual 'heavy, blunt instrument.' The Lauderdale cops think it might have been a sledge hammer."

"Jesus . . ." I breathed, "Smitty Mackilson. What was he doing down in Florida?"

"That's the trouble," Vantil said. "We don't know. I spoke to him last Thursday. He was in Rossinger, a little town on the Sound, just below Kings Park. There are a lot of marinas around there. We had just been notified about the disappearance of the *Princess*, a 40-footer, from the King Ross Marina. Mackilson went out to look around."

"Did you tape his report?" I asked.

"No," Vantil said unhappily. "I didn't. It was an informal report, only lasted a few minutes. He said he thought he might be onto something. I asked him what it was. He said he'd rather not say until he checked it out. It was the last I heard from him. The Lauderdale cops called last night. Now it's your headache. Here's the file—everything we've got. Claims on boats that have disappeared, apparently stolen, are now nudging the six-million mark. It's got to be stopped."

"It will be stopped," General Davidson growled in his best "damn-the-torpedoes" style.

"Have you brought the Coast Guard in on this?" I asked Vantil.

"Oh, God, yes," he said wearily. "You know how many registered pleasure craft there are on the Eastern seaboard alone? I can't quote you the exact figure, but it's hundreds of thousands. The Coast Guard has sent out bulletins to every dock and marina in the country, describing the lost boats. Not a nibble. But you know how easy it is to change a boat's appearance? A new coat of paint. Change the name and registry number. Forge false papers. Take off a wooden cabin and replace it with a canvas cockpit cover. Or just cover the wood with canvas. Yank out deck chairs or put them in. Make a double outboard into a single. There are a hundred ways. And this is the middle of summer. You think every harbor master or marina owner is going to take the time to check every strange boat he sees against the Coast Guard bulletins? Forget it. Here's the file, including my transcribed notes of my last telephone conversation with Mackilson."

I took the fat file from his outstretched hand.

"Poor Smitty," I mourned. "I didn't know him long but I really liked the guy. Competent. Fast. And a good sense of humor. I think he had a wife and two kids."

"Did he?" Cyrus Vantil said.

A true claims man.

There was little in the file I could use. Three men had worked on the case before Mackilson took over, and all of them had drawn blanks. There were no signs of damaged or burned boats; they had simply disappeared. Most of them vanished from April to September when boats are in the water, but a few had disappeared from shipyards during the lay-up season.

The most recent disappearance, as Vantil had mentioned, was the diesel-powered *Princess*, a 40-foot inboard, from the Rossinger marina. I went over everything and figured I could do no better than retrace the dead man's path; I threw some jeans and beach togs into a bag, got into my ancient wheezing Pontiac and headed for Rossinger.

All the way out there I kept seeing an 18-pound sledge hammer coming down on a man's skull and Adam's apple. Chunk, chunk, chunk. And pleasant dreams to you, Smitty Mackilson, wherever you are . . .

I spent two days nosing around Rossinger, and at the end of the 45 hours all I had to show for my trouble were a peeling forehead and baked-red forearms. I talked to three guys who had been questioned by Mackilson. One of them was the owner of the King Ross Marina. But none of the three could help a bit. Mackilson had been trying to trace the *Princess*. All they could tell him was that it had been tied up in Berth 112 in the evening. In the morning it was gone, and the owner—who had slept ashore—was screaming bloody murder.

Finally, I gave up and got out of the sun

in a lusciously air-conditioned bar that was one of the shoreside pleasures offered to mariners by King Ross. I was on my second bourbon-and-water when a gink a few stools down from me at the bar turned in my direction. He looked about one year younger than God and was wearing an old, sweat-stained captain's hat.

"Purty sight," he said, gesturing toward a picture window at the end of the bar. It gave a view over the entire marina and most of Long Island Sound. You could see power boats zipping along, heading out from their berths or coming in slow to tie up. And you could see sailboats scudding along under a nice breeze, some with their spinnakers set.

"Yeah," I said grumpily. "Purty sight."

"Lot of money out there," he went on. "More boats every year. Purty soon they'll be clawing up each other's backs. Oh well, I reckon they all got insurance."

"Yeah," I muttered, hardly loud enough for the old guy to hear me. "With old Barnes Casualty, I suppose."

But the codger's hearing was better than I thought. "Some with Barnes," he nodded affably. "Some with Keystone. Some with Oberleigh. A lot of outfits getting into marine insurance these days with all these boats—"

I jerked upright, knocked over my drink and made a disgusting puddle of bourbon on the bar.

"What?" I yelled at him. "What did you just say?"

He turned and looked at me equably, not turning a hair.

"You some kind of a nut, son?" he asked—rather reasonably, I thought, considering my conduct. "I said some might be insured with Barnes and some with Keystone and some—"

I tossed a double-sawbuck on the bar. "Buy him whatever he wants," I yelled at the bartender, motioning toward Captain Ahab. Then I made a dash for the phone booth.

I got Cyrus Vantil in a minute. Thank God for area codes.

"How many other marine insurance companies are in your field?" I demanded. "Outfits that specialize in pleasure boats."

"At least 20," he said in his wispy voice. "None as big as Barnes, of course, but there's Oberleigh and Keystone and—"

"Forget it," I said. "When did your boats start disappearing?"

"If you had read the file carefully," he began, "you'd know—"

"All right, all right," I groaned. "About two years ago your losses took a sharp rise. What about the other companies in the field?"

That shook him. I heard a sharp intake of breath.

"Just a moment, please," he said, quietly enough. "I have the figures in the file. It'll just take a moment—"

He was right; it just took a moment to discover that no other company had shown a record of losses comparable to Barnes'. Oh, their losses had increased, but at a rate justified by the growth of pleasure boating. "My God," Vantil said. "My God."

"Yes, my God," I mocked him, happy to shake him up. "I told you Smitty Mackilson was a competent guy. A helluva lot more competent than you, me or General Davidson. How late does your Records Office stay open?"

"It closes at five," he said dully.

"The hell it does," I snapped. "It stays open all night tonight, if I say so. I'm out in Rossinger. Give me three hours to get in. Meanwhile, you have your Records dig out the last known addresses of everyone who has resigned or been fired from Barnes during the past three years."

But he wasn't as dumb as I figured; claims men never are.

"You mean any resigned or discharged personnel who left a forwarding address in Fort Lauderdale? Or who listed nearest relative as residing in Fort Lauderdale?"

"Yeah," I said disgustedly, "that's exactly what I mean. It shouldn't take long. In fact, it shouldn't take any time at all. Because I'll bet you a hundred Yankee dollars that your Records men prepared exactly the same list for Smitty Mackilson about a week ago."

"Oh, oh, oh," he groaned. "How could I have been so stupid?"

I liked him for that. A lesser man would have said, "How could *we* have been so stupid?"

"I'm coming in," I told him. "Can you call my office, speak to Davidson and have him lay on transportation for me to Lauderdale, first available. And a hotel or motel reservation; whatever they can arrange. Soonest."

"I'll take care of everything," he said. "God, why didn't I see it?"

So there you have it, in a king-size nutshell: the reason why I was basking in the sun-warmed breezes of Fort Lauderdale, watching half-naked blondes do perfect dives from the high board, and smelling my city-green skin roasting to a blackened crisp.

But it wasn't all fun-and-games, of course. I was surrounded by the case. A few blocks behind me was the Intracoastal Waterway, and I was convinced the stolen and camouflaged boats had been sailed down that route to be sold in the Fort Lauderdale area. South of the chaise longue on which I lolled was Bahia Mar, possibly the largest and most beautiful marina on the Atlantic, berthing both private pleasure craft and commercial fishing boats. It was a sight to see.

And farther south and west were all the marinas, shipyards and repair docks in the Hollywood–Lauderdale–Pompano Beach area. To say nothing of the private yacht clubs. The whole place was a boatman's delight, and I could understand the workings of Smitty Mackilson's mind.

He jumped to the conclusion that the whole caper was a "get even" scheme against the Barnes Marine Casualty Company before I did. He got a list of discharged or resigned employees of Barnes for the past three years—ginks who might conceivably have a deep, aching grudge against Barnes.

Smitty figured the boats would be taken south to the crowded anchorages of Florida via the Intracoastal Waterway. Where else? Take them north and the not-so-busy marina owners and harbor masters of New England would spot them for sure.

So Smitty guessed his best bet would be the Fort Lauderdale area. He winnowed the list given him by the Barnes Records Department, took out the names of ex-employees who had given their forwarding address as being in Fort Lauderdale, or who had listed next-of-kin in that area.

Smitty guessed. And because he guessed right, somebody played the bongos on his skull with an 18-pound sledge. I should never be so right.

My flight landed in Miami. I checked in with the Triple-I's Miami office (professional courtesy) and made arrangements to have them tape my daily reports and send them on to Manhattan via teletype. I rented a car, a late model Honda, and set out for Lauderdale, which is, incidentally, known to the natives as Liquordale, for obvious reasons.

I had three names on my list. The first was a guy in Hollywood. It took about 20 minutes to cross him off; he had died a year previously from choking to death on a tooth-pick. Sounds silly, doesn't it? But it happens more often than you think.

The other two on the list were in the Fort Lauderdale area. Jake Spencill had been discharged as a claims agent from Barnes 30 months ago when he was caught taking kick-backs from claimants. About two weeks after he got the boot, a secretary, Alicia Hofstra, had resigned, giving "poor health" as her reason for quitting Barnes and retiring to sunny Florida.

I had been at the Shade-Rest Motel in Lauderdale about an hour when I got a call from Cyrus Vantil, the demon claims man of Barnes.

He said, "I have evidence of a hookup; between Spencill and Hofstra. Need a second?"

He had dug out the fact that the discharged Jake Spencill and the resigned Alicia Hofstra were buddy-buddy. "Need a second?" was his way of asking me if I could use some help, say a claims man from Barnes to go out for hot coffee.

I thanked him and said no.

I spent my first two days at the Shade-Rest getting settled and answering the questions of the curious—and there were a lot of them—as to what I was doing in Lauderdale. I was a stockbroker in Manhattan and was thinking of opening a branch office somewhere in the Miami–Lauderdale–Palm Beach area. I was looking for an office location, a place for my branch manager to live, and maybe a boat big enough to entertain good clients when they came south for the winter. Everyone nodded understandingly.

On the morning of the third day I gassed up the rental car and headed for the address given on the separation report for Jake Spencill. I only got lost three times, but when I found the place, it hardly seemed worth the trouble. It was a sleazy, run-down motel, only about five miles from the beach, and I hoped the wallpaper was strong; the stucco was flaking off in such big, bald patches that the place looked ready to collapse any minute.

I talked to the owner, who was sucking on a cold cigar. He told me he hadn't seen or heard of Jake Spencill in almost a year. He had left suddenly, owing three weeks' rent, and—quite naturally—had left no forwarding address. Zero.

Alicia Hofstra was something else again. Her last address was a smart, spanking-new motel on a street only two blocks from the beach and only four blocks from my own motel. But Alicia didn't live there anymore.

The owner looked like a retired stripper— or maybe a madam who had decided to go straight in her old age. Her hair looked like it had been dyed with peppermint candy, and her body was encased in some nutty kind of an elastic bra, stretching in all directions, and a pair of purple jeans so tight they must have been painted on her. Between bra and jeans was a jutting roll of sunburned flesh like a circular bratwurst. Delicious.

"Hi, honey!" she flamed at me. "Looking for a room? I've got just the thing for you. You'll love it here. A real swinging crew. Every Saturday night we—"

"Whoa, whoa, wait a minute." I held up a protesting hand. "I don't want a room. I'm looking for Alicia Hofstra. I've got a letter for her from her mommy up no'th."

"Ain't that a shame?" she said regretfully. "I've got so many wonderful, beautiful single gals staying here, and I just can't seem to snag a male single. You're a disappointment to me, honey. Who was that you mentioned?"

"Alicia Hofstra," I repeated. "Doesn't she live here?"

I must have said something funny because

all those soft inches began jiggling and writhing.

"Alicia?" she gasped finally. "Hell, no, honey, she don't live here anymore. Not since she hit it big. Hey, you know, you're the second guy been asking for Alicia the last week or so."

"I suppose the first guy was tall and skinny and had an Adam's apple that bobbed up and down when he talked?"

"Yeah, honey, that's the cat. You know him?"

"A friend," I said briefly. "But what about Alicia?"

"Didn't you hear, honey? She hit it big. She's Princess Irene now. Dances at the Delly-Mar. That's on the coast, just south of Pompano Beach. She's a big hit, honey. She does this African bit. Comes out in a wild thing or two—not too much, you understand—and this cat behind her is beating the drums like crazy. The snowbirds eat it up."

"The snowbirds?"

"The tourists, honey. The northerners who head down this way right after the first snowfall. Say, Alicia baby ain't in any trouble, is she?"

"Absolutely not," I assured her. "I just

want to say hello to her from her folks up north. I'll certainly look her up at the Delly-Mar."

"You do that," she said, clamping a hot, damp hand on my arm. "And if you're not doing anything Saturday night, come around. Y'hear? We have all kinds of fun. Like we have this poolside cocktail party. Men in one team, women in another. You gotta hold a lemon between your chin and chest, and you gotta pass it to a girl without using your hands. You understand? Just using your chin and shoulder. The first one to drop the lemon loses. Lots of laughs. Lot of fun,"

"Sounds like," I nodded. "I'll certainly try hard to be here Saturday night. I'll even bring my own lemon."

The flesh started heaving again.

"You do that," she chortled, "You do that. Can always use an odd man."

"I'm as odd as they come," I assured her.

She was practically hysterical with laughter when I left. That's what I like—a good audience.

I postponed tracing Jake Spencill and Alicia Hofstra, now Princess Irene, for another day. Instead, I spent 24 hours visiting or calling every shipyard and yacht broker in the Lauderdale area. I gave them all the same song-and-dance. I was a stockbroker from New York, thinking of relocating in the area, looking for a boat I could use to entertain snowbird clients.

I described the boat I wanted—and, of course, it was the *Princess* that had vanished from the King Ross Marina in Rossinger, Long Island. I wanted a 40-foot Shelfly cruiser with a fiberglass hull, twin diesels, sleeps six. Completely equipped with electronic gear, an electric head, flying bridge . . . the works. I didn't care what color it was or how the cabins were decorated; I intended to have the whole thing re-done anyway.

Everyone was most interested, took my phone number and assured me they'd check their files immediately. So much for dangling the bait.

I called the Delly-Mar and discovered that Princess Irene was still featured in their "Belly-Laugh Room." Shows at 12:00 and 2:00 A.M. Did I wish to make a reservation? I hung up.

I got up to Pompano a little after midnight. I turned my Honda over to the jockey and got a plastic tag in return. I watched him park it, a refugee from the Daytona 500. All I heard was the squeal of brakes and

169

the dull thud of crumpled fenders. The world's full of nuts.

The Belly-Laugh Room was just what you might expect from the name. Not as big as "Le Grand Ballroom," but just as sick-making. A phony English-pub-type bar with about 20 tables crammed in. A small stage opposite the bar. A guy with bare feet playing an electronic organ. Fake shields and escutcheons nailed to the thin paneling on the walls. So dark you had to light a match to find your drink. Paradise.

I shouldered my way into the screaming crowd at the bar and finally got a Jim Beam. I tasted it and immediately ordered another double, straight. They must have been using thimbles for shot glasses. I got one good drink out of the three shots.

The guy playing the organ faded away. A spotlight came on, focused on the curtains of the miniature stage. Suddenly the uproar quieted. Everyone was still, looking toward the drawn curtains.

"And now, folks," a sepulchral voice said from the loudspeaker, "the Belly-Laugh Room is proud to present its feature attraction—the incredible Princess Irene! Let's have a big hand for the Princess, folks!"

I know it sounds corny. It *was* corny.

Cheap bar. Lousy drinks, Third-class hotel. An audience of half-drunk tourists. Imitation English-pub-type bar. The whole bit.

And then *she* came on. And she was pure class, genuine. She sparkled like a diamond in a nest of rhinestones. And everything seemed right.

She couldn't have been much more than nine feet tall, with arms and legs about five feet long. She was stretched out, elongated, with as much shape as a wooden clothespin. She didn't have a face; she had a living mask: eyes stretched upward at a slant, lips full and cold. It was scary.

She wore some kind of a kooky African amulet around her neck. It had a jewel in the center that looked like a third eye. It damn near hypnotized me. I forgot to sip my bourbon—so you know she was really strong medicine.

Behind her was a guy dressed in rags. His head was down; he never did look up. All he did was touch and stroke and thump and pound about a dozen different drums laid out in front of him: primitive African drums. The son of a bitch was good . . . so good. He scared you. You felt it as much as heard it. He got this slow, deep rhythm going and you wanted to take off your clothes, bite the head off a live chicken and bay at the moon. I mean this guy was fantastic! He stroked a beat out of those nutty drums that touched something down deep inside of you, something you never knew was there . . . or had forgotten.

She stood there for about three minutes, not moving. When the curtains had parted, the audience had drawn one deep, collective breath—"Ahhh," like that. After that, there was complete silence except for the drums. No one moved or even blinked.

She began to move. It was nothing frantic, nothing orgiastic. She seemed to waver, to sway, to bend and flow to that primitive drumbeat. Then, in a moment, the rhythm and her body were one—throbbing and fluttering and the incredibly long fingers were signaling in the air and the slender legs were waving like ribbons.

I don't know what the hell it was supposed to be—a savage war dance or a fertility rite or what. But she had us. She had us all, men and women. No one could take his eyes away, and no one could help but feel the deep, dark, primeval stir of her dance.

She did it expressionlessly, coldly, and it was like she was saying. "You think you're civilized? You think you like to wear clothes?

You think that nine-to-five job is the real you? Here's what you are, actually, underneath. You're an animal, just out of the ooze. You'll kill for food and kill for a woman. Watch me, animal. This is what you are!"

I tell you, she shook me up.

The drums faded away. That long, long brown body slowly stilled. The hair stopped waving. The smooth stomach stopped fluttering. The curtains came together. There was very little applause. But it took at least ten minutes before the monkeys were chattering again, and the waiters could hustle drinks.

"I want to see her," I said to the bartender, palming him a bill. "Now. Backstage."

"Get in line, buster," he smirked, taking the sawbuck. "There are only a few hundred ahead of you."

I passed him another ten.

"You're moving up," he said. "You're getting right to the head of the line."

I slipped him a twenty, wondering how I'd account for it on my swindle sheet.

"The winner!" he said, "You've just reached the very top of the heap. Outside, around the corner, service entrance, down the hall, first door on your left. Tell her Sollie sent you."

She was wearing a dark brown dressing gown, exactly the color of her skin. She had let me in when I told her Sollie had sent me. She was all business. She told me I could pick her up about 2:30, after her second show. I nodded. I think we might have exchanged perhaps a dozen words.

You know how I spent those two hours? I walked down to the beach, took off my shoes and socks and carried them, rolled up my pants and waded through the shallow surf, wet sand and damp seaweed for a mile up the beach and back. I watched the moon zip up out of the Atlantic Ocean, and I saw the lights of a cruise ship. It was cool and damp and blowy. I wondered if I'd ever be young again, and I kept hearing those damned drums. It wasn't a good two hours. I saw too much of what I am and what I'd probably become.

She came out of the service entrance, carrying a little plastic suitcase. Her drummer came right after her. He didn't even look at me, just turned, got into a white Porsche and pulled away with a chirp of tires.

She gave me her address, a cooperative apartment in a new development on the border between Pompano and Lauderdale. I made a few false turns, but we finally got there. Dark. Quiet. An outdoor swimming pool shimmering in the moonlight.

Her place was small but neat. Very clean. She went in to shower and told me to mix drinks. She came out in a white, terry-cloth robe, a big man's robe, the kind they give you in the better Parisian hotels. She was tired; that was obvious. Those dances took it out of her.

"Stay the night?" she asked finally, after finishing half her gin-and-tonic.

"I don't think so," I said. "Regretfully. Nothing personal."

"So. What *do* you want?"

"Why did you leave Barnes Marine Casualty Company?"

God, she was good. She didn't flick a hair.

"Poor health," she said. "Isn't that what it says on my resignation?"

"That's what it says," I nodded.

She got up and moved around the room slowly. I watched her very carefully indeed. I figured she'd be fast, and I had seen the muscles. If she had reached for a vase or a poker or anything else, I'd have been all over her like a wet sheet.

"Who are you?" she said finally.

175

"A friend of Smitty Mackilson," I said.

"Mackilson, Mackilson?" she repeated. "Don't believe I know the gent'man."

"Oh, you know him. And don't give me your pickaninny accent, baby. It just isn't you. I saw you dance. Do you like fairy stories, sweetie?"

"Love them."

"Listen to this one. All guesswork. Not an iota of evidence to back it up—or, at least, none I'd tell you about."

"I'm all ears, yummy."

"There's a guy named Jake Spencill. A good insurance claims man who goes sour and gets canned for tapping claimants. There's a girl named Alicia Hofstra, a secretary at the same agency where Spencill works. They're close, real close. How am I doing so far, Princess?"

"Tell me more, sweetums."

"After meeting you, I'll bet the kickbacks were your idea. Spencill went along with it to keep you. What man wouldn't?"

"I do thank you, sir."

"So . . . he gets canned. So you do some thinking and resign. Your home's in Florida, you like the hot sun. The hell with those cold, sleety, nasty New York winters. Right?

You've been doing some dancing. You figure you can make a connection down here."

"Do tell."

"More important, you're a brainy chick and you don't like the deal Spencill got from Barnes. What about heisting boats up north —boats insured by Barnes—changing their appearance, sailing them south by the Intracoastal Waterway and selling them in the Fort Lauderdale area, where boats are being bought and sold every day? Sounds good? You bet! Try it on one boat first. That works fine. Two boats, three, a dozen, 20. No problems. Except that now you're in business. A regular corporation. You've got a staff and schedules and all that crap. Guys are picking up the boats from Long Island marinas. Other guys are changing them around in little coves on, maybe, the Connecticut shore. Other guys are bringing them south. Other guys are selling them here. My God, it's like General Motors—a great big thriving corporation."

"How you do go on, sugar-boy," she laughed.

"So you cost Barnes almost six mil in the last two years. That's big biz, baby. But you need a cover. So you become Princess Irene, queen of the jungle. Perfect. And you enjoy it."

I got to her for the first time.

"You bastard!" she spat out. "White bastard!"

"The hell you say. I'm beginning to get a tan. So now there's only one question to be answered."

"You'd like me to tell you where Jake Spencill is." She smiled, mockingly, back to her control.

"That's right."

"Won't tomorrow do?"

"Afraid not, Princess. By the way, did you know the last boat you listed was called the *Princess?*"

"I didn't know . . . no. Fascinating, isn't it?"

"Enthralling. Where's Jake Spencill?"

"Tell you in the morning?"

"Now."

I told you she was good. She had been slumped down in an armchair. She stood up languidly and that robe fell away. It wasn't just her—though she was a royal flush—it was the memory of the dance and the drum rhythm still beating away like a nervous tic in my mind.

God, she was beautiful. I could under-

stand why Jake Spencill did what he did—
what a junkie would do for a shot of horse,
what a wino would do for just one more sip
of muscatel.

She was like a very tall boy, but she had
things no boy ever had. She faced me for a
moment and then, almost contemptuously,
turned away and curled up on the couch, her
back turned toward me. She was so sure, so
sure . . .

The black hair fell across neck and shoulders. There was a ribboned curve from
shoulder to waist to hip to thigh to ankle. I
couldn't resist it. You couldn't resist it.

Once she knew she had conquered I
wouldn't have blamed her if she had lain like
a log and let me fuss with her. But she was
too smart for that. She was still acting the
primitive female—or was it an act? I'll never
know.

I had no sooner touched her than she
came alive, burning, bursting. I knew she
was trapping me. In my mind I knew it. But
sometimes you can know the right thing to
do, the smart thing to do—and you go right
ahead and make a fool of yourself. I always
have and I guess I always will.

I just shoved Barnes and Jake Spencill and
the stolen boats way back to a far, dim cor-

ner of my mind. Up front, in light and heat, was her silky body coiled around me like a rope. That's all I knew or wanted: the feel of her, and the taste of her lips, and the perfume of her flesh.

This was a wild one, so knowledgeable, so practised, so expert at love-making that I had to cram a knuckle in my mouth to keep from screaming. She turned me upside down and inside out. I never want to go through that again. I never want to lose control like that again, to be reduced to one small, searing nerve end that flickered rawly like a candle flame. And she kept it burning . . .

God knows what time it was when she finished with me and let me pass out or go to sleep—I don't know which. But I felt her body draw away, her hands stopped, and a big, heavy black iron curtain came down in my mind—clank!—like that, and I was out. It was deep and dreamless. I don't think I moved a muscle all night.

When I finally awoke I could see hot sunshine coming through the slatted blinds. She was standing, dressed, in front of a full-length door mirror, putting on long, dangling earrings.

The guy was sitting in the armchair, staring at me. I figured the gun lying in his lap was a .38 Police Special. It might have been a .32, but I think my first guess was right. I sat up in bed and pulled up the sheet to hide a little of my nakedness.

"Mr. Spencill, I presume," I said.

He turned his eyes away to look at her.

"We'll have to," he said. "This mutt hit every shipyard and yacht broker in the area, describing the *Princess*. He's probably got a message from Bixby & Boyd waiting for him at his motel right now. They know me as the owner. So we'll have to put him down."

"All right," she shrugged indifferently. "How do you want to work it?"

"My wagon's across the street. You get it and drive up in front. I'll walk him out and get in the back with him. We'll drive out to the beach and find some place. Maybe they won't find him as fast as the other one."

Interesting to hear your own demise planned in such detail.

She nodded and went out the door. When it closed, he picked up the gun, stood and moved back a few steps.

"Get dressed," he said tonelessly.

He was too far away to make a play for the piece. I got slowly out of bed, being careful to make no sudden moves. I pulled on my shorts, trying to stall for time, trying

181

to grab a few extra minutes . . . to keep alive a few extra minutes. I was pulling my socks on when I heard the station wagon pull up in front and she beeped the horn a little.

"Faster," he said. "Hurry it up."

Screw him. I wasn't going to rush to my own funeral, and I was sure—well, *fairly* sure—he wouldn't blast me in that apartment house. Too much noise. And bloodstains are so hard to scrub off a shag rug. So I took my time . . . slowly, slowly pulling on my pants and shirt, getting zipped up. Finally I got the break I was hoping for: she got impatient and came back inside.

"What's the hold-up?" she asked.

He motioned at me with the gun muzzle. "He's stalling."

I stopped dressing and smiled pleasantly at her. "Princess," I said, "let's you and me dump this guy."

"What?" he said. "What?"

"Use that tiny, tiny brain of yours for a minute, Princess," I went on, still staring at her. "You think if you put me down, that'll be the end of it? The hell it will. The trip is over, baby. Everyone off."

"What are you talking about, sweetums?" she asked, puzzled.

"You think if I disappear nothing will happen? Or maybe they'll send a *third* agent and you'll smash his skull, too? Forget it! They'll send a platoon of cops, half the FBI, the Coast Guard and maybe a regiment of Marines. Don't you think I've been filing daily reports? Your address is in New York right now. They've got your names, they've got your photos from your job applications at Barnes, they know how the whole setup works."

"Don't listen to him!" he shouted. "Don't listen to him! We'll make a run for it!"

But I was getting to her. I could see it in her eyes, a deepening of awareness and maybe the beginning of fear . . .

"Run for it?" I said. "That's a laugh! Where to? Cuba or the Iron Curtain countries? That's your only chance. Otherwise they're going to track you down and stretch you. Maybe insurance companies don't pay their agents a helluva big salary, but they don't like it when they get pounded to mush with a sledge hammer. Then they'll spend a lot of money and a lot of time. Princess, you've had it. It's finished, kaput, done with."

"Yeah?" she murmured. "Tell me more."

"Alicia," he hissed in horror and amazement.

"Dump him, Princess," I advised her. "Let him take the big stretch. You didn't know he was going to kill Mackilson, did you? And he handled the sledge, didn't he? You were practically an innocent bystander. Dump him, baby, and make a deal. Maybe you'll get five and be out in two. You're a young woman, and the world's full of rich fools. You can be a big help—names and addresses of everyone in the ring, how the whole thing was set up. Let him take the drop. You've got a whole life to live. You don't want to live it on the run. You'll never have any fun that way."

She turned and stared at him speculatively, like a farmer looks at a sick horse he knows he's got to kill.

"Makes sense, sweetums," she said softly. "Makes a lot of sense. I do believe the music has stopped."

"Alicia," he said, almost choking, "you don't . . . you can't . . . don't listen . . . after what I've done for you, after what I've done?"

She moved close to him and put the long, slender fingers of one hand against his cheek. She looked deep into his eyes.

"But the music has stopped, sugar-boy. Don't you dig? Like the man says, the trip is over. Everybody off. They won't stretch you, baby. You'll get a good lawyer and he'll get you off. You'll be out before you know it and we can be together again."

She pressed her body close to him. I knew it had worked for her a hundred times before, that she had used her body to tease and tantalize and torture him until he would have jumped off a cliff if she said, "Jump!"

But he wouldn't jump now.

It sounded like a cannon in that room, and the impact of the slug smashed her back and sent her spinning onto the floor. He moved over close, his mouth working, pulling the trigger again and again and again, watching the invisible fingers pluck and jerk at that incredible body. There was very little blood.

He was still clicking away when I reached him, chopped at his neck under his left ear, caught him as he fell and eased him into the armchair. I made the calls that had to be made. When I heard the sirens, I slapped his face lightly until he came around, dazed and shattered. I helped him to his feet.

"Let's go, sweetums," I said.

Death of a Model

You probably saw her naked body a thousand times, and never saw her face or knew her name. She was the most successful nude model in Manhattan, posing for everything from earth-moving machinery to the latest in armpit deodorants.

As a matter of fact, her face wasn't bad—not beautiful, but pleasant. It was her body that was so incredible, and early in her modeling career she realized it was her trump card. In fashion and glamor modeling, new faces come and go. A beautiful model, if she's lucky, can last for perhaps three to five years. Then art directors and clients start screaming, "I've used her before. She's old! Don't you have anyone new?"

So models' agents cross the 23-year-old "has-been" off their list and look for someone new, fresh, just in from Oak Elbow, Nebraska, or Ox Eye, Arizona. It's a rough business, and if you're going on your face, you better make it while you can—because it ain't going to last.

A girl with a good body who's willing to pose in the nude is something else again. Usually her face doesn't show; she's just a body. And if she keeps the flesh in shape, she can charge anywhere from $150 to $450 an hour—offering a neck and shoulder to a cosmetic ad, a hipline to a girdle ad, legs for hosiery or a hair-remover, etc.

Wanda Giles was a hip chick and caught on to the facts of modeling life a few months after she arrived in New York from St. Cloud, Missouri. She had a body that photographed like money in the bank—solid, tight-skinned, full, with good muscle tone and a natural grace that made you want to snap your suspenders every time you saw her on glossy paper. It didn't matter that you never saw her face or learned her name; all that mattered was that sexy envelope of skin, bursting with youth, juice and vitality.

After five years of work she made the down payment on a converted brownstone on East 83rd Street, rented out the top two floors and took over the bottom two, sharing them with her brother, a scenic designer she brought in from St. Cloud to keep her company. At the time of her death, she had been modeling for more than ten years and was still getting jobs. She worked out of the Allied Model Agency on East 38th Street, and if you wanted her for a magazine ad or a TV commercial, you had to reserve her services at least a month ahead—but maybe that was a put-on.

Her brother, Timothy, found her body. They had fixed up a second-floor back room that she used as a kind of gym. She was a nut on yoga and stretching exercises, worked out at least an hour a day, and when Timothy got a call from Allied, saying that Wanda Giles hadn't shown up for her first assignment of the day, the brother went looking for her in the gym.

The floor was covered with black linoleum, and she was lying face down, arms and legs outstretched, her long blonde hair pulled over to one side and tucked under her shoulder.

Later, the brother told the cops he thought at first she was in a "yoga trance" or had fallen asleep while doing her relaxing exercises. No, he didn't think it unusual that she was naked; she never wore anything while exercising.

He called her name loudly, but she didn't

respond. He touched her bare shoulder, and she was cold. His first thought, he said, was that she'd had a heart attack. Then he rolled her over.

As I said, you never saw her face—and it's a good thing you didn't see it then. Someone had done a job on it with that famous "blunt instrument," plus a double-edged knife. The Medical Examiner counted 37 individual blows and slashes . . . and then gave up. It didn't make much difference anyway; what had killed Wanda Giles was a well-aimed knife thrust into her left breast.

I work for the International Insurance Investigators, and we do claims investigations for a number of small or overworked insurance companies. We got called into this one by LaFrance Insurance Co., a small outfit with headquarters in St. Louis. LaFrance had insured Wanda Giles for $150,000, double in case of accidental death. The beneficiary was Timothy Giles, the fancy brother.

The boss of the Triple-I, Lt. Gen. Lemuel K. Davidson, USMC (Ret.), tossed this one in my lap with a grimace of distaste.

"Nasty," he said, shaking his head. "I don't like the manner of death. Killing is one thing, but slashing and pounding in a maniacal fury is something else again."

"What have the cops got, sir?" I asked him. The case was already three weeks old.

"Not a great deal," he said, glancing down at his notes. "The body was found at about 10:30 A.M. The ME fixes the time of death at anywhere from three to five hours previously; he can't be any more exact than that. The brother, who found the body, says he was in his basement studio all morning, from approximately 9:00 A.M. until he got the call from the model agency a little before 10:30. He says he heard nothing. The top two floors have tenants—two apartments on each floor —and two young married women were home, one on the third floor, one on the fourth. They, also, heard nothing. Here are photos of the body . . ."

He tossed two 8 × 10 glossies across his desk to me. One showed Wanda Giles lying naked, face down, as she must have been when her brother walked into the gym. The other photo showed her face up. I swallowed hard.

"Thanks a lot," I said.

The General nodded grimly. "It's all yours," he said.

"Thanks a lot," I repeated, trying very hard to keep my breakfast down.

I went back to my broom-closet office, got

out my desk pint of Jim Beam and had a heavy shot. That photo of Wanda Giles' face had really shook me. Someone not only wanted to kill her, but to unload a world of anger and madness. What could she have done to deserve that kind of treatment?

After my stomach stopped fluttering, I called Timothy Giles, explained who I was and made an appointment to meet with him that afternoon. As a matter of routine, I called Records and asked them to run a check on the bank accounts and debts outstanding of Wanda and Timothy Giles. As an afterthought, I also asked for a balance sheet on the Allied Model Agency, the modeling outfit that handled Wanda.

I got down to Allied a little after noon, and the waiting room was filled with the greatest collection of young feminine pulchritude I've seen since the last time I was in Mama Loo's in Honolulu. They were all bright, leggy birds, skinny as ballpoint pens, but with great legs and chirpy looks on their indecently youthful and innocent faces. They were all dressed in extreme stuff—leather and see-through blouses and beaded bands around their long hair—and they were all carrying these big portfolios with a sampling of their photos.

Five pairs of eager eyes looked at me when I came in, then froze as the owners realized that a guy who wore an unpressed, five-year-old suit, scuffed moccasins and a brocade tie that held the history of almost every lunch for the past six months couldn't possibly be a client. And I sure as hell wasn't a model—unless the magazines devoted to horror stories were hard up for villains.

A receptionist finally came out of an inner office. She was all teeth, a faint mustache and had probably seen Halley's Comet twice. I asked to see the boss of the joint, told her it was a "private, personal" matter and handed over my potsy. She grudgingly agreed to take it in, was gone a few moments, then came out to say that Mrs. Amanda Blake would see me now.

I figured Mrs. Blake had been a model herself at one time. Now she was getting a little long in the tooth, but her face had that kind of hard bone structure that improves with age. Nothing sags; the skin just gets tighter and tighter. When I came into her private office, she stood up to hold out her hand. She was almost as tall as I was, broad-shouldered, with long arms and legs. The jaw was definite and the hands were strong.

A real no-nonsense woman, handsome rather than pretty or beautiful.

She gave me a chair alongside her desk, then sat down and swung her swivel chair around to face me and crossed her legs. Very, very nice indeed. I'm a Leg Man myself, and I can appreciate the finer points of well-shaped feet, slim ankles, full calves, dimpled knees and the beginnings of firm thighs. She had them all. *Dear* Mrs. Blake.

She told me she and her husband, Arnold Blake, owned and managed the Allied Model Agency. He was out lunching with a client. Yes, Wanda Giles had been one of their girls, one of their *best* girls. They were devastated by her death—not only because of the loss of income it meant for them, but because they both liked Wanda very much, liked her as a human being, a friend. I understood, of course?

I told her I understood.

I asked her about boyfriends. She said Wanda went out with several men, to dinners, the theatre, ballet, etc. She had been engaged several years ago, but that hadn't worked out, and since then Wanda had played the field. I asked for the name and address of the man Wanda Giles had been engaged to. She finally dredged up the name of the guy from her memory, Warren Hyde, but told me that the last she heard, he was designing men's shirts on Carnaby Street in London. So . . .

Since the method of Wanda's murder looked like a real grudge thing to me, I asked Amanda Blake if Wanda had ever gone out with any married men. Paydirt . . .

Big business of fishing cigarettes out of her top desk drawer, holding the cigarette in fingers that trembled slightly as I leaned forward to light it, then leaning back to blow a big, dramatic plume of smoke at the ceiling.

"Yes, Mr. Lannihan," she said, not looking at me. "I know of at least one married man Wanda dated. My husband—Arnold."

I said nothing, just watching her as she puffed nervously at the cigarette.

"You seem like a competent man," she said, smiling mirthlessly, "and I'm sure you'd find this out from other sources eventually. My husband began seeing Wanda—outside of office hours, I mean—about three years ago. You understand that she's been with us ever since she came to New York. But I believe their—their affair started about three years ago. As usual, the wife is the last to know. I learned about it six months ago. He said he would break off the—the relationship. And I believe that he did. I believe that he has been completely faithful to me for the past six months."

Then she looked up at me . . . stonily, challenging.

"Do you believe me?" she asked.

"Why not?" I shrugged. "In matters like this, I trust a wife's instinct."

"Will it be necessary for you to question my husband about this?"

"I can't promise you anything, Mrs. Blake. Perhaps it will. Perhaps it won't. I can't guarantee anything. You understand?"

"Yes," she said miserably. "Of course."

She got up, turned her back to me, walked over to the window, pulled the curtain aside and stared out. Then I got a good look at her. Any guy who would cheat on that must be nuts. Her body wasn't Wanda Giles', but in its own way it was just as good—tight, strong, hard, with muscled haunches and thighs pressing out against her wool skirt. She had a very slender waist cinched in with a wide, black leather belt. I saw her for a moment in profile as she turned back to me. The breasts weren't enormous under the white silk blouse, but they were firm and shapely.

"Now what?" she asked.

"Nothing," I said, "I may call your husband for an appointment, or I may call you for more information. You've been a big help."

"I bet I have," she said bitterly.

When I walked through the outer office, the waiting models didn't even bother looking up. They probably thought I was selling costume jewelry wholesale, door-to-door.

The Giles' brownstone on East 83rd Street was a handsome building, painted a sand color. There was a small flight of steps leading down to the below-street-level apartment with a chic white sign over the basement doorway that said: "Timothy Giles—Scenic Design." The main stairs led upward to a small, wood-paneled lobby with the names of the tenants in brass mailboxes, with a bell button under each.

I pushed the first one, that said simply "Giles," and waited a few minutes. Nothing happened, and I pushed again. I heard a voice yell, "Down here!" I looked out the glass entrance door. There was a guy standing on the lower staircase motioning me downward. This was, I decided, Timothy Giles, at work in his basement studio.

He was a vision. Foulard Apache scarf . . . deep purple shirt . . . silk slacks in an electric green shade . . . a brocade tie for a belt . . . no socks . . . snakeskin moccasins . . . heavy, glittering rings on three fingers of each hand . . . a gold chain-link wristwatch around one wrist . . . a silver chain-link identification bracelet around the other . . . and a thick, fruity cologne.

His studio ran the length of the house, and there was a beautifully designed Japanese garden out in back. Walls and ceilings were painted a flat white. Furniture was mostly black leather on chrome frames. That stuff costs money—big money.

We sat at a cocktail table that was a single slab of milky white marble supported by a rusty black cast-iron frame. We sat in those crazy modern chairs, so comfortable you wanted to curl up and sleep. He was sipping a green crème de menthe on-the-rocks and offered me one. I declined, and he offered nothing else. So that was that.

I looked around the main studio room and politely admired the sketches pinned to the walls. They seemed to be rough drawings for ballet scenery, done in fast water colors. He didn't bother thanking me for my interest.

We got down to the nitty-gritty, and I took him through the events of the morning on which he had discovered his sister's battered corpse. The night before he had worked very late in his basement studio. As a matter of fact, he had been doing preliminary sketches for the backdrops of a new musical hopefully planned for Broadway.

He had gone upstairs to his first-floor bedroom at about 2:00 A.M. He slept until 7:00, then got up, showered, dressed, had some breakfast and was back down in the studio by 9:00. He hadn't seen or heard his sister Wanda moving about.

"I was so anxious to get at my work again," he told me. "It was so important to me."

He thought Wanda might have an early appointment or might be up in the gym doing her yoga exercises. It wasn't unusual. They sometimes went two or three days without seeing each other. They each had their careers and their own lives to lead . . .

When Allied Model Agency called about 10:30, saying Wanda hadn't shown up for her first job of the day, he had trudged upstairs to see if he could find her. He found her all right—lying face down on the gym floor. Then he turned her over.

"That must have been quite a shock," I prompted.

"Ill-making," he said, fitting another cigarette to his holder. "Positively ill-making."

Just before I left, he asked if I knew when he could collect the 300 grand on his sister's insurance.

So I went back to my fleabag hotel, ordered up a hot pastrami on rye and a container of black coffee. I wolfed this mess down, then got rid of the aftertaste with a noggin of Beam. I mixed a second drink, kicked off my shoes, propped up the pillows and flopped on the bed. I drank and thought, thought and drank. Nothing . . . except that whoever did Wanda Giles in must have hated her something awful. That poor dead face . . . blah.

The office, which never sleeps, called me at about 7:30 P.M. They had the financial checkouts I had requested . . .

Allied Model Agency got a good report. The Blakes owned a thriving business, had money in the bank, paid their bills promptly and had personal savings and checking accounts that seemed reasonable in light of the dough they were making.

Timothy Giles had never had a savings account, as far as could be determined. He presently had a bit under $300 in a checking account. Until Wanda's estate was settled, the lad would be a bit strapped since rents from the tenants on the two upper floors of the Giles' house on East 83rd were being paid to a bank pending settlement of the estate.

Wanda herself, at the time of her death, had about two grand in a savings account plus about $700 in a checking account at another bank. Not much for a chick who owned a brownstone on the East Side. Also, about five years ago Wanda had almost $90,000 in cash deposited in a savings bank, and more than $8,000 in a special checking account. But then constant withdrawals had reduced this amount to its emaciated status at the time of her death. She had closed out a brokerage account, surrendered a safety deposit box and generally gave every evidence of losing a helluva lot of loot, considering what her income must have been.

I slept on that.

The next day I called the Allied Model Agency, made an appointment to meet with Arnold Blake—and ran into a real hardnose. The man wouldn't talk. Period. He was a big, rangy guy with the look of a heavy drinker—splotchy complexion, sagging paunch, a breath you could chin yourself on.

He saw me in the private office, and the luscious Amanda wasn't present. I braced him with hints that we knew about his "relationship" with the slain Wanda Giles, and he didn't blink an eye. He said that had all ended six months before Wanda's death.

I asked to look at the books to get an idea of how much Wanda had been making, and he just laughed at me. I asked him if he knew of any other guys—single or married—she had been seeing, and he just said, "No," and let it go at that.

It was a wasted morning.

I devoted that evening to talking to the four tenants in the upper two floors of the Giles' brownstone. I learned nothing more from them than I already knew—except that they all swore that Wanda and brother Timothy were "very devoted." That's the exact phrase all four used—"very devoted."

The week was shot, and I didn't know much more than when the General first gave me the file. I did know that Wanda Giles had gone through a good piece of change in the five years her brother had been in town—but what did that prove? I knew her brother was broke—so what? Most people in the theatrical field are. I knew Wanda and Timothy were very devoted, and that Arnold Blake had had an affair with Wanda that ended about six months before her death—he and his wife claimed.

A lot of nothing.

The General asked for a report. I told him to tell LaFrance Insurance that the investigation was continuing. A few days later he braced me again. LaFrance was getting itchy and wondering how long they should stall. I told Davidson to tell the company to stall as long as we told them to stall.

"But what are you *doing?*" he demanded.

"Thinking, sir," I told him—and he hung up with a bang that almost cracked my ear.

Actually, believe it or not, I *had* been thinking. And drinking mucho Jim Beam. I had been thinking if Timothy Giles had it in him to murder his sister and slash her face to ribbons.

Naturally, in cases like this, the beneficiary is the first suspect. But I had been doing some additional checking on Timothy with contacts I have in the theatrical field, and I couldn't see him as a killer. From what I learned, he was strictly a no-talent who moved around on the fringes of Broadway and never made it. He just didn't have it.

But he had told me he wanted to invest in a new show. Maybe killing his sister would be his one chance of breaking into the world of the theatre, not only as a scenic designer but as a producer as well.

But could Timothy batter his sister's face like that? The upstairs tenants had assured me that Wanda and Timothy were "very devoted." Unless it was a sex thing with him. But that didn't make sense. All Wanda's beauty was in her body, not her face. If Timothy wanted to destroy what attracted men to her, he'd have slashed her body. But her body was relatively unharmed . . . only her face was destroyed.

"Well, Lannihan?" the General demanded every day.

"Tell LaFrance to stall," I advised him every day. "I'm thinking, sir."

BANG! would go his telephone.

It didn't come in any great flash of inspiration. It came slowly and painfully, and I think I got my first hint while I was going over that business of Timothy Giles' possible motives, and why he should want to slash his sister's face rather than her body. Why would *anyone* destroy a victim's face in that manner? I think I almost shouted aloud when I asked myself that question. It was the key.

I spent the noon hours of the next three days standing across the street from the Allied Model Agency. The first day Amanda and Arnold Blake came out together, at about 12:30. I tailed them to a nearby restaurant and left them. The second day Amanda came out by herself. I followed her on a rambling shopping tour of Fifth Avenue department stores, then dropped her. On the third day, Arnold Blake came out by himself. I followed him for about two blocks. Then he finally got into a cab. I doubled back to the agency and whisked upstairs.

"Mrs. Blake," I said to her, after I got into the private office, "your husband is involved in this thing."

"Oh, God," she groaned, and buried her face in her hands. "I was afraid of it. I was afraid of it."

So I lied in my teeth and got her to show me the income ledger of Wanda Giles. She had a little over $9,000 the first year she modeled in New York. It rose steadily and dramatically until, by her seventh year, she was grossing almost $150,000 a year. That's a lot of loot for skin, bone and meat—but I guess she was worth it.

Her earnings had taken just as dramatic a drop in the last three years. In the past 12 months, her earnings were just under $35,000.

"How come?" I asked Mrs. Blake.

"She was getting older," she said dully. "Younger girls were coming along. Clients wanted new girls—they always want new girls. They started saying, 'What? Wanda Giles again? Haven't you anyone new?' "

"And did you have anyone new, Mrs. Blake?"

"Well . . . there was . . . we . . . did . . ."

"What was her name, Mrs. Blake?"

"Cynthia. Cynthia Traven,"

"What happened to her?"

"She went home."

"Where's home?"

"I don't know. I think she said California. Somewhere in California."

"She went home—and you haven't heard from her since?"

"Yes. That's right."

"A blonde?"

"Yes."

"With a body like Wanda Giles'?"

"Yes."

"Did you get a visit from a cop from the Missing Persons Bureau, Mrs. Blake? I can check this out, you know."

"Yes. We got a visit."

I left her then, sobbing, her face and shoulders down on her desk. They weren't in on it, but they knew, they knew . . .

I called the Missing Persons Bureau and identified myself. The guy on the phone read me the sheet on Cynthia Traven. The physical description could have been that of Wanda Giles, they were that much alike.

I was eager now, almost panting. And I was as furious as I've ever been in my life, thinking what they had done to that girl—a girl I had never met and never would.

I went over to the precinct that handled the original run on the case. I got hold of a Detective-Two named Walter Macready. I laid it all out for him.

"Oh, God," he said.

And then he said several other things that can't be printed.

We picked up two uniformed men in a car and drove over to the brownstone on East 83rd Street. One of the buttons circled around to the back. The other one came in with us.

Timothy Giles was dabbling away at one of his stupid water colors in his basement studio.

"Gentlemen!" he said heartily. "And what do I owe the honor of—"

"Where is she?" I said.

"What?" he said. "What?"

"Your sister," I said, and suddenly I was

tired, defeated, sick of the whole business and just wanted to see it end. "She's somewhere. Living in the attic? The French Riviera? Back home in St. Cloud?"

"What are you talking about?" he screamed.

"Cynthia Traven worked in a government agency for awhile before she became a model," I told him dully. "The Missing Persons Bureau told me. Her prints are on file. Do you want us to dig her up?"

"I didn't do it," he yelped. "I swear I didn't do it. It was Wanda's idea. Wanda suggested it—I swear it. I needed the money. She needed money. It was all going out. Nothing was coming in. I'll tell you where she is. I'll help you catch her. It's her fault. I didn't touch the girl. I wouldn't touch a woman. Wanda used the knife and the hammer. It's Wanda's fault. I tell you she—"

Then Detective Walter Macready groaned and hit him once. I turned around and walked out.

The Girl in the Office

I read about the case in the newspaper about a month before it was dumped in my lap. I remember that at the time I was reading it, I was grinning like a maniac. Listen, I can admire professional workmanship whether it's on my side of the law or the other.

What happened was that these two cool cats, wearing the uniforms of the Tracy Armored Car Service, walked into the uptown branch of the Tanners Commercial Bank and asked for the cloth bag containing $450,000 that was to be delivered to Tanners' downtown branch. The bag was ready for them and handed over after the men signed the required receipts. They then walked out with the dough.

About an hour later the two real Tracy guards showed up and asked for the bag. It was about then, I figured, the head teller at Tanners felt a cold finger prodding at him.

As I read about this beautifully planned and executed bit of thievery I was thinking that it had obviously been engineered from inside the bank or from inside the armored car service. The two hoods had to know the bag was ready for delivery and at what time. They had to know the proper uniforms, the code word (if there was one) and the papers they'd have to sign before the money was handed over. So I figured someone inside the bank or inside Tracy's was in on the scheme.

Having solved the whole brouhaha in three seconds, I promptly forgot about it and turned to the sports section.

But I didn't get rid of the Tanners heist that easily. A month later there it was again, all mine. I work for the International Insurance Investigators. We do claims investigation work for a long list of blue-ribbon insurance agencies who don't have the claims investigators to do the job for them, or whose claims men seem to be getting nowhere.

That was the case with Bensen Casualty, the outfit that insured the two branches of Tanners Commercial Bank. They were on the hook for the purloined 450 G's, and their claims men couldn't find a hole. So they came to the Triple-I, and it became our headache. We had never handled a case for Bensen before, and Lt. Gen. Lemuel K. Davidson, USMC (Ret.), the boss of my outfit, didn't have to spell it out for me: if we saved Bensen the nasty chore of paying out the $450,000, or showed them how to recover it, we'd have another client to add to our list. Big deal.

As I say, the con was a month old before it got to me. I took the big, fat file back to my broom-closet office, kicked off my shoes, got out my office bottle of Jim Beam, a few paper cups, locked my door and settled down to a lazy afternoon of reading. A month had passed; the trail was cold; there didn't seem much reason to get in an uproar over the whole thing.

As I dug my way through the file I was impressed once again with the cool nonchalance of the two guys who pulled the job, According to the bank witnesses, they exhibited no nervousness whatsoever. They were wearing what were apparently legitimate Tracy Armored Car Service uniforms. They smiled politely, asked for the $450,000 to be delivered to Tanners' downtown branch and knew exactly what papers to sign and where. They were out of the bank in two minutes with the loot. No one saw whether they drove away in a Tracy armored car or a private car or escaped on pogo sticks or what.

The clerks and tellers at Tanners didn't suspect a thing until the two real Tracy men showed up an hour later.

I then went through the reports of Bensen Casualty's investigators. It was obvious they figured this for an inside job, just as I had. Someone in Tanners or in Tracy's had to be in on it to alert the bad guys when the delivery would be ready and when it could be picked up.

So the claims men had sniffed around both the bank and the armored car company. All personnel who had been even remotely connected with the shipment of the cash were investigated back to their days in the cradle. Even the presidents of both companies were checked out. People were tailed for weeks; bugs were put under desks; tape recordings were made of men's room conversations—and it all added up to a big, fat zero. Nothing.

I sat there, sipping my Beam, and wondering if it would be worth my time to go back over the ground covered by the Bensen gumshoes, interview all those people at the bank and at the delivery service. I decided not to. The Bensen claims men obviously knew what they were doing; if they had uncovered nothing, there was nothing to uncover.

Okay, Lannihan, I muttered to myself, let's try something the Bensen men didn't go into. The uniforms. Where did the two crooks get those official Tracy Armored Car Service uniforms?

Having arrived at this momentous question, I closed up shop, went home, slept for two hours, then woke, showered and shaved. I called a little creampuff I know, a chick with the body of a dancer and the brain of a gnat, and we went out and worked our way through a great slab of rare roast beef while she told me, between mouthfuls, how everyone in show biz wanted to get her into bed.

The idiots. Didn't they know that all they had to do was feed her?

The next morning, refreshed mentally and physically, I called General Davidson and asked if he'd assign one of the new men to checking out every theatrical costume renter in the city, trying to find one who might have rented two uniforms around the time of the robbery, uniforms that resembled those used by the Tracy Service.

"Good idea," the boss man growled over

the phone. "Should have been done before. Good thinking, Lannihan."

"Thank you, sir," I said modestly.

"Onto anything?"

"Not a thing, sir."

"Get humping, man, get humping," he shouted and slammed down the phone.

That's what I like: a pat on the head, then a kick in the teeth.

I couldn't believe anything would come from the costume rental checkout; it was hard to believe any crooks would be so stupid as to rent their uniforms. So I went down to Tracy and talked to their Chief of Security.

He was a tall, thin guy, almost totally bald, with a nervous tic that kept his right eyelid fluttering. When I told him I was investigating the Tanners Commercial Bank heist, I thought he was going to burst out crying.

"Not our fault, not our fault," he said rapidly. "But we are involved, we are involved."

I figured if he was going to say everything twice. I'd be there all day. I asked him how long Tanners had been a customer of the Tracy Armored Car Service.

"About ten years," he said, "Yes, about ten years."

It went on like that. I'll cut it in half and tell you what I learned.

Tanners was a commercial bank established almost 100 years ago in a section of the city called The Swamp. Originally it had been the center of the leather trade, hence the title "Tanners." As many of the wholesale leather dealers moved uptown, Tanners kept their original location but also opened an uptown branch. They only had the two banks.

Heavy cash shipments were made between the two Tanners branches, by Tracy armored car, at least once a week. The purpose was to cover big cash withdrawals from one branch or the other, or maybe to lay off part of a big cash deposit in one branch. On the morning of the robbery there was absolutely nothing unusual in the request from the head teller of the uptown Tanners for a delivery to be made to the downtown branch.

"When did you first hear of the robbery?" I asked Tracy's Chief of Security.

"About 11:30," he said. "Yes, about 11:30. Right after our men—our real men—showed up."

"About the uniforms . . ." I started, and

then I realized this guy might have some funny mannerisms, but he was no dope.

The moment he heard about the guys in Tracy uniforms who had swiped the cash, he ran a check on all uniforms issued by his company. Each Tracy guard was issued two uniforms. The guard came to work in his street clothes, changed into uniform in the company locker room. When his uniform got dirty enough to be sent to the dry cleaner, he switched to his second uniform.

After hearing about the robbery, the Tracy Chief of Security had counted the uniformed guards he had on duty that morning. He had then opened every locker with his master key and counted the uniforms stored there. He had then gone over to the outfit that did the Tracy dry cleaning and personally counted the uniforms in for cleaning. The total was exactly right; no uniforms were missing.

"Who does your dry cleaning?" I asked him.

"Smith-Stone," he said. "Yes, Smith-Stone. They're over on 33rd Street. That's 33rd Street."

"Thank you," I said. "Thank you."

Now he had me doing it!

Don't ask me what the hell I was doing

visiting the store that did Tracy's dry cleaning, but I had no other leads and it seemed to me the whole thing revolved around those official Tracy uniforms and how the crooks got hold of them. And besides, I knew of a great tavern not too far from Smith-Stone's location that served mutton chops and dark ale. That was reason enough to make the trip.

I had my chop and ale before I went over to Smith-Stone—which turned out to be a smart move because the guy behind the counter might easily have spoiled my appetite. He looked like a moth-eaten gorilla, with grey, wiry hair sprouting out of his nose, his ears, from the backs of his hands, out of the unbuttoned collar of his shirt and, for all I knew, from the soles of his feet.

He also looked directly into my eyes as he talked to me. Very sincere. He also talked without moving his lips. It all spelled ex-con, though I didn't want to put the slam on the guy without checking.

In any event, he had little of interest to tell me. He picked up the soiled uniforms from Tracy headquarters. He cleaned them and then he returned them. All the dry cleaning was done on the premises. He had never lost a Tracy uniform; none had ever been stolen.

"How long have you had Tracy as a customer?" I asked him.

"About a year," he growled in a voice like a constipated bullfrog.

So that was that. Just for the hell of it I called our Records Department at the Triple-I and asked them to run a credit check on the Smith-Stone Dry Cleaners on 33rd Street and, while they were at it, see what they could dig up on the bullfrog, Ernest Stone, who apparently owned the business.

It seemed a little early to go home to my fleabag hotel and start drinking. So I went into a nearby saloon and started drinking. Why fight it?

I sat in a dim booth and made little wet circles on the table top with my highball glass. I went back over the Tanners heist in my mind, trying to think of anything I could try that I already hadn't, any angle to explore that no one had yet considered.

No inspirations. No light bulbs suddenly blazing in the air over my head. Nothing. Three drinks later I wandered out into the late afternoon sunshine and started looking for a cab. By this time I was over on Madison Avenue. There was a bank on the corner, and an armored truck was making a delivery. It wasn't from Tracy. I watched the guards carry in sacks of money, and I wondered why the bank needed the cash right then—for a big loan, to cover salary checks . . . why?

Maybe it wasn't a good thought, but it was the only one I had, and it was one no one else had asked: Why had the uptown branch of Tanners been ready to transfer $450,000 to their downtown branch on the day of the robbery?

So I called the uptown Tanners and finally got through to a vice president. He wouldn't talk—which didn't surprise me. So I called Lieutenant General Davidson at the Triple-I. He called the president of Bensen Casualty, our client. Bensen called Tanners and got the information. Then it started in reverse: Bensen called Davidson at the Triple-I, and Davidson called me at the number of the phone booth I had given him. The phone company did very well that day.

Tanners had planned the cash shipment because a client of their downtown branch had requested a $450,000 short-term loan in order to make a cash purchase of imported hides. The company requesting the loan was the Carney Leather Import Co., 2075 Charles Street.

Then I did go home, fell onto my lumpy bed and corked off a few hours. I was awakened by a phone call from Records. They said they were having trouble finding the name of the owner of the Smith-Stone Dry Cleaners. It wasn't Ernest Stone; he was just the manager of the place. But they had discovered that Smith-Stone had repaid a $60,000 bank loan in full about two weeks ago.

I thanked Records and asked them to keep digging on the owner of record. I also asked them to find out what they could about the Carney Leather Import Co., 2075 Charles Street.

I went down to the office early the next morning and began to lean on people. I had that itchy feeling that this thing was about to break open, and all I had to do was push a little. I pushed the new man who was checking the costume rental agencies, and by noon he had covered the last one on his list and was ready to swear no one had rented armed guard-type uniforms in the last six months.

Also by noon I got a check from Records on Ernest Stone, manager of the Smith-Stone Dry Cleaners. As I suspected, he was an ex-con. He had tripped twice on armed robbery, the last time serving more than seven years. His probation officer said that, as far as he knew, Stone was walking the arrow. Oh sure.

Then I got the credit report on Carney Leather Import Co. Up to about a year ago, they had done fine. But then old man Carney died, and the business went to his son, David Carney. Since then it had gone downhill, and the gossip around The Swamp was that young Carney was living too high, and bleeding the company to do it. However, the credit check did reveal that after losing the loot, Tanners Commercial Bank dug up another 450 G's to lend Carney, and the loan was repaid promptly, with interest.

And finally, the Triple-I man who had gone downtown to the Bureau of Records in an effort to trace the ownership of the Smith-Stone Dry Cleaners called in his little nugget. The owner of record was Miss Gerta Stone.

Her address was given as 2075 Charles Street. Banzai!

I could have called a meeting of General Davidson, the president of Bensen Casualty, the Chief of Security of Tracy and the vice president of Tanners Commercial and laid it all out for them. But I knew better than that. What I had in mind was illegal, and I couldn't involve these upright citizens. That's why I was making my big five-figure salary—because I knew enough to act first and tell them about it later.

I have a guy outside the company who does some bug work for me occasionally. As a matter of fact, he works for the phone company, so it's easy for him to get into places. He hauled his equipment up to Carney Leather Import Co., told the office manager he was making a preliminary inspection prior to bringing in a new trunk line. The office manager didn't know what the hell he was talking about, but he was a trusting soul and let my man check and inspect the switchboard, the connection box and all the phones in the place.

My guy left about three hours later, leaving behind him a sweet little gizmo in David Carney's private phone. It not only tapped incoming and outgoing calls but picked up all the conversation in the room. All this it transmitted to a truck I had parked down the block. I could monitor the bug via a loudspeaker if I wanted to, or I could use a voice-actuated tape recorder. I wasn't about to sit in a hot van eight hours a day, so I opted for the recorder. Besides, I had things to do.

I got two guys from the Triple-I to help me, and we worked fast in the next few days. We got a photo of David Carney (from the United Association of Independent Leather Merchants, no less!), and I went to visit him at his office on Charles Street. I said I wanted to sell him some insurance and was given the brush-off by his personal secretary, Miss Gerta Stone.

She was a big, ripe, hefty chick, almost as tall as her ex-con brother, but not as hairy. She also impressed me as having a brain or two, and I figured she had worked out the details of the caper with her brother's professional assistance.

Oh yes . . . the Triple-I man who was tailing David Carney reported that he seemed to be spending most of his nights in Miss Stone's apartment. It didn't take long to discover that checks from Carney Leather Import Co. were paying the rent.

Meanwhile I was going through mug books down at Police Headquarters, looking for guys Ernest Stone had worked with in his Armed Robbery and Breaking & Entering days. I even went back to his prison days and got photos of the cons he was known to have been palsy with, including a cell mate.

I took all my photos to the uptown branch of Tanners, and the tellers who had handed over the bag of cash to the phony guards positively identified one guy, a bruiser named Jeff McCarthy whose home was in Chicago, It figured they'd bring in outside talent for a hit-and-run like that.

The only thing that bugged me was how David Carney and Gerta Stone knew that the downtown branch of Tanners would request that cash shipment from the uptown branch. A VP at Tanners did some checking for me and discovered that two other similar loans had been made to Carney in the past year. They were promptly repaid. All the loans were made on the 30th of the month when the downtown Tanners had a heavy outflow to cash salary checks. Carney & Co. just kept trying until they hit it. I had a feeling they also had a tip-off from someone in the bank or someone in Tracy's.

I could have made a fortune selling copies of those tapes of David Carney's conversations with his private secretary when they thought they were safe in the sanctuary of his private office. Hot? Man, we should have been using asbestos tape! She had that guy so juiced-up that he probably would have gone along with whatever she suggested, even if he wasn't hurting for money.

Then I held my grand meeting, with Davidson, the guy from Bensen Casualty, the Tracy representative and a VP from Tanners Commercial Bank who had persuaded David Carney and Gerta Stone to come along, on the pretext that this was to be a business meeting to discuss the financial affairs of the Carney Leather Import Co.

I went into my song-and-dance, laying it all out for them, naming names and giving details on how they managed it—taking the Tracy uniforms out of the dry cleaner's and returning them immediately after the heist had been made. I told them how Ernest Stone, Gerta's brother, not only supplied the uniforms but brought two of his friends in from out-of-town to make the actual snatch.

As I talked, Gerta got red and Carney got white. After the shock wore off a bit, they began spluttering, so I started a play-back of one of their tapes. I was going to play the real wild one where she was obviously sitting in his big leather swivel chair and he was . . . oh well, you know these executives and their private offices.

But I was kind and good and considerate

and only played the tapes where her brother called Carney to report that I had been snooping around, and Carney told him to calm down, there was nothing to worry about, the robbery had gone off without a hitch and no one suspected a thing.

Most of the money was already spent, so it didn't look like Bensen Casualty would get much back from their insurance payment to Tanners. But, after the Carney Company was liquidated, Bensen might not do too bad. It would take years of litigation to settle, but money doesn't get rusty.

We turned them over to the fuzz, who had already picked up Ernest Stone on a complaint issued by Tanners. A pick-up order was out on Jeff McCarthy of Chicago, and we left it to the cops to discover the identity of the second guy.

We finally got them all out of General Davidson's office. He wandered over and poked a finger at the stacks of tapes I had accumulated.

"Highly irregular, Lannihan," he growled. "In fact, highly illegal."

"It certainly was, sir," I agreed. "Robbing a bank like that . . ."

He sighed.

The Curse of the
Upper Classes

You only make a bad mistake once in my business. Then you never make a mistake of any kind again—because you're on a tray in a horizontal icebox with a red tag tied to your big toe. The tag explains the details of your mistake—lead perforations through various portions of your carcass, perhaps a swift knife slice here and there, maybe a piano wire noose making a tight ascot around your throat—or it could be as primitive as a fandango performed on your groin, with steel heel plates.

I was on an industrial arson case down in Baltimore, and my mistake was following the suspect into a blind alley. He was a little wrinkled-up guy, known as Ernie the Torch. I never figured he'd go hard, but I had no sooner turned the corner into the alley than there he was, icepick in hand, coming at me like a linebacker for the Los Angeles Rams.

So I sighed, got out my stick and put two through his chest. You could have covered the holes with a Kennedy half-dollar. But before he crumpled at my feet he slid the pick between my ribs and I sat down suddenly in the alley, wondering if I was going to die, and wishing I hadn't sent Internal Revenue their check that morning.

Well, I didn't die—but breathing was quite a chore for awhile. They finally got me on my feet again, and General Davidson gave me two weeks off to get back to what he called, in his Lt. Gen., USMC (Ret.), style, "fighting trim."

General Davidson took over as director of the International Insurance Investigators after Mac Brady walked in on three guys playing dominoes with gold bars and asked them, politely, to try to touch the ceiling. It was a famous case involving a Brazil-bound plane and some nutty revolutionists who wanted the dull, burnished bars to buy cap pistols and cherry bombs and stuff like that. You probably read about it in the papers. Instead of hoisting them, as Mac Brady requested, the three clunks went for their hardware. Mac never dogged it in his life, and by the time the smoke cleared two of the hijackers were dead and the third was coughing up his lungs on the garage floor. Mac was dead too, a serene smile on his face. He was much man.

So Gen. Lemuel K. Davidson was elected —a tough, hard-bitten, go-by-the-book retired Marine. He ran a tight ship and there was no doubt who was boss. If he wasn't liked, as Mac Brady had been, he was respected or feared. Anyway, he did the job and he had brains, so no one complained.

He called me in the morning I got back to the Triple-I's Manhattan headquarters and tossed a file across his desk at me. He didn't ask me how I was feeling, but I guess he had seen the medical report and was satisfied.

"The client is the Arcana Insurance Co.," he started rattling in his machine-gun fashion, his voice as smooth and velvety as a wood rasp. "It involves the payment of $500,000 to the beneficiary of Jerome K. Baxter, an industrialist who recently died following a diabetic coma. You'll find all the details there. This is an HWC case."

In our agency HWC means "Handle With Care." It doesn't mean that violence can be expected; all our cases are like that. But it means the principals involved are high muckamucks in the social, business, theatrical or political worlds and that more than ordinary discretion should be observed.

General Davidson said he'd discuss the Baxter case with me after I had a chance to go over the file. He nodded and I got up and resisted a terrible temptation to click my heels and salute. Sometimes these military types bug me.

I took the file back to my office—slightly larger than a broom closet but not much—packed my favorite Petersen Shamrock with Brindley's Mixture and started reading.

The facts were simple enough. Jerome K. Baxter came out of the Navy a radar technician. On borrowed funds he started a factory making electronic components. He must have been a sharp operator because when he went to the Great Stereo Set in the Sky at the age of 54, he was worth well over $8,000,000, and his company was valued at about 20 times that.

He insured with Arcana for $500,000 at the age of 32. Ten years later, he was found to have diabetes and was put on one tablet of oral insulin per day. He took his medicine faithfully and there was no history of further attacks up to the time he died. His doctor was Dr. Warren G. Bemott of Garden Grove. That's on Long Island, a few miles from the

Baxter home—a rather lavish suburban lay-out that included a private stable for two horses.

Jerome Baxter had a 16-year-old daughter at the time of his death. But his wife had died four years before, and after a suitable period of grief, consisting of two weeks, he had remarried a divorcée who worked in the main office of his electronics empire. Need-less to say, she no longer worked there. Her name was Magda Baxter, and she was—or had been—a Hungarian refugee.

On July 9, Baxter, his wife and his daugh-ter had driven up to their secluded retreat in northern Vermont. Both wife and daughter testified that Baxter had taken a sufficient supply of his diabetes pills with him. Both women also testified that he took them regu-larly for the first three days they were up there, gulping the pill down each morning at the breakfast table.

On the fourth day, Baxter went into a diabetic coma. His wife drove into the near-est town, really a crossroads with a general store, a gas station and a dozen homes. Magda described the emergency to a local deputy sheriff, a farmer, and he apparently used his head. He called the nearest State Police barracks, told them what had happened and asked for a helicopter.

Baxter was rich enough to be known even in Vermont, and a police chopper was dispatched forthwith. They flew him to Boston. His personal doctor, Warren Bemott, flew up from Garden Grove. But in spite of everything that could be done, Jerome K. Baxter shuffled off this mortal coil at 8:23 A.M. the following morning.

As I say, the facts were simple enough. But I could see what was nudging the guy who has to sign the checks at Arcana Insurance. Here's a man with diabetes who's been taking his pills faithfully for years and years, He goes on a trip, takes his pills right on schedule—according to wife and daughter— but collapses and dies. And Arcana is out $500,000. The facts might be simple but they also had a slight smell of something spoiled.

General Davidson gave me ten minutes of his valuable time and we discussed how I should handle it. It was agreed that I'd go to Garden Grove and operate out of there. The usual written report filed every day. The usual "rigorous effort" to hold down on unnecessary expenses. Like eating.

I departed Davidson's office, called a motel in Garden Grove to get a room and headed home to pack. On the way out I stopped by Records and asked for a complete run-down on Jerome Baxter, Magda Baxter and Terry Baxter, the 16-year-old daughter. Also on Dr. Warren Bemott. The dossiers would be mailed to me at the motel.

I'll say one thing for that motel; the food in the restaurant may have been lousy, but the room was worse, They had central air-conditioning turned on full-blast, with no controls in the room to regulate it. You could have hung sides of beef in there with no fear of spoilage.

I woke the next morning with a dandy cold—the whole bit: sneezes, runny nose, watery eyes. After a steaming hot shower I figured I might live, dammit, and called the Baxter home. A Brooklyn accent said, "Baxter residence," and I asked for the be-reaved widow. While I was waiting, I heard that cautious little click that says someone is lifting an extension phone.

The widow came on. Low voice. Husky. Sexy. I identified myself and asked if I might come out and talk to her. She said sure, come right ahead. Just a trace of accent. Twice she asked me to speak louder and confessed she was a bit hard-of-hearing. She gave me directions on how to find the Baxter place. I crawled into my five-year-old Pontiac, still sneezing, and got moving.

The Brooklyn accent answered the doorbell wearing a neat little uniform of black and white, just like a French maid but with considerably longer hemlines. Too bad. What I could see looked good. She led me into the "library" to wait for Magda. The house looked as big from the inside as it did from out on the graveled driveway. A big, expensive, well-kept-up joint that smelled of money.

I was wandering around, staring at book titles, when a door across the room opened, a blonde head thrust in and went, "Psst!"

"Psst, yourself," I said. "You must be Terry Baxter."

A body followed the head into the room, and if cops could read minds, I'd have drawn 20 years for what I was thinking. This had to be the hottest 16-year-old package I've ever seen. Buttock-length hair, so blonde it was almost white, and perfectly straight and gleaming. A tight, white cotton tee-shirt, the contents bouncing so I knew they were real. White short-shorts, so snug and so short that I couldn't believe she could ever sit down in them.

And the legs! Long and tanned and smooth. Hard where they should be hard and soft where they should be soft. And curved. The whole body should have been declared illegal.

After awhile I happened to notice the face. Typical young, rich girl's face: good teeth, revealed by a short upper lip, a vapid expression, empty blue eyes, a little snub nose. Pretty—but nothing. So? With legs like those, who needs a nose?

"Yes," she whispered, "I'm Terry Baxter. And you're the man from the insurance investigators."

"And you're the one who listened on the extension," I said. "Don't you know that's not polite? Why are you whispering?"

"I don't want her to hear," she said, coming close, so close that I backed up a step. "I've got to talk fast. Listen, you better look into this."

"Look into what?"

"My father. His dying. You know? There's something phony."

"What's phony?"

"Something. Magda and Dr. Bemott. There's a thing there."

"A thing?"

"Between them."

"Oh."

"And don't let Magda tell you she's hard-of-hearing. She's not. It's just an excuse to get closer to men. You know?"

At the moment she was practically glued against me, hissing her information into my face.

"Yes," I said, "I know."

"Good," she said. "You look into it. If you want to talk to me outside the house, you can contact me through Bobby. He works in the drugstore in Garden Grove."

"Bobby. Drugstore, Garden Grove," I nodded wisely in my most mysterious secret-agent manner. "Got it."

She pressed my arm.

"I like you," she whispered. "I trust you."

She shouldn't have. She wouldn't have if she'd known what I was thinking. I watched those short-shorts bob away from me as she went out the door. I was sweating—but it may have been my cold.

Magda Baxter was a ripe brunette, in her late 30s I guessed. Short-cut hair, dark eyes, moist lips, flesh that looked like it would bruise easily and heal slowly. Sexuality hovered about her like an expensive perfume. I could understand why Jerome Baxter only waited two weeks after the death of his first wife before marrying this Hungarian pastry. It was all I could do to keep from reaching out and touching the velvety softness of her neck, the shadow in her shoulder, revealed by a low-cut blouse. Then there was an incredibly narrow waist, nipped in with a wide, patent-leather belt. Swollen hips encased in black suede. Stiletto-heeled shoes. She didn't walk; she flowed; she oozed—all soft flesh, melting.

She came up close to me and again apologized for being hard-of-hearing and too vain to use a hearing aid. She pouted and smiled and dimpled, and I felt myself grinning at her like an idiot and bobbing my head like one of those crazy Chinese dolls.

We sat close to each other on a leather couch, and I took her through the whole story—her late husband's diabetes, his routine of taking one insulin pill per day, the trip to Vermont, the fatal coma, what she did and what others did. She answered all my questions in her slow, husky voice, and I learned nothing new.

"Where did your husband keep his pills?" I asked. "Bottle? Box?"

"He bought them 50 at a time," she said. "The bottle was kept in the medicine cabinet in the bathroom adjoining the master bedroom. My husband used a pill box—an antique silver box of some value. Each week he put in exactly seven pills. The box was kept in a drawer in a sideboard in the dining room. He took from it one pill each morning."

"I wonder if I could see the bottle of pills in the medicine cabinet?" I asked. "Also, I'd like to see the pill box, which, I presume, he took to Vermont with him."

She hesitated a moment, then leaned toward me, her soft breast brushing my arm.

"Pardon?" she said, pronouncing it like the French.

"The pill bottle," I said in a louder voice. "Also the pill box."

"The bottle certainly," she said. "I'll give it to you before you leave. But the silver pill box my husband owned has disappeared."

"Disappeared?"

"Yes. I looked for it to take with us on the helicopter to Boston. I thought he might need the pills. You understand? But the box had disappeared. After his—his death, I returned to the lodge in Vermont with Terry, to pick up our luggage. We made a more careful search. We could not find the pill box."

I nodded, keeping my face expressionless.

"Tell me, Mrs. Baxter, how well do you get along with Terry?"

"Very well. Of course, there was at first a certain amount of friction. A young girl who adored her father. And her mother. And then a stepmother. You understand?"

"Of course."

"But recently things have been going better. Much better."

"Do you like Terry, Mrs. Baxter?"

"I love Terry, Mr. Lannihan. I see in her exactly the problems and frustrations and worries I had when I was her age."

"And does Terry love you, Mrs. Baxter?"

Something strange came into her eyes, a veiling, a shadow, It was like a half-opened Venetian blind coming down over a clear window.

"I suggest you ask Terry, Mr. Lannihan," she said softly, rose, and that was that.

I departed the Baxter ménage with the deceased's bottle of pills in my pocket. Back at the motel, I shook out about five of the pills into an envelope and tucked it into my jacket. The bottle and remainder of the pills I wrapped carefully and mailed off to the Triple-I headquarters, asking for a quick analysis.

Meanwhile, I had some mail of my own—

the dossiers I had requested on Jerome, Magda and Terry Baxter, and on Dr. Warren Bemott. The reports had been culled from every source—insurance examinations, credit ratings, Social Security, charge accounts, etc. I learned nothing new about the dead man. Magda, according to her insurance examination, had 50 percent impairment of hearing in her right ear. Terry Baxter, about a year ago, had been picked up in a general police raid on a teenage party at which, it was suspected, pot was being smoked. She was released for lack of evidence, and no charges were brought. A photostat of a newspaper report of the raid was attached for my bemusement. I was mildly intrigued to learn that a certain Robert Habbler, employed as pharmacist in a Garden Grove drugstore, had also been picked up in the raid.

The report on Dr. Bemott showed two suits of malpractice, which could mean nothing at all. He was 38, a bachelor, earned (or at least *declared*) almost $225,000 a year and had the reputation of being a ladies' man. Most of his patients appeared to be women.

His reception room looked like $225,000 a year—all chromium and black leather. And behind a mahogany desk, just a bit smaller than a Ping-Pong table, sat a blonde in a white nylon uniform. She must have cost a healthy chunk of those 225 G's.

She looked up at me and smiled. I looked down at her and smiled. But she was smiling into my eyes, and my eyes were smiling into the gaping neckline of her white uniform. There was something wonderful on display there. It wasn't Picasso, but it was a work of art—all tanned and rosy and bulging.

"I called Dr. Bemott for an appointment," I finally said, in a voice that sounded strange and strangled even to me. "My name is Lannihan."

"Ah, yes, Mr. Lannihan," she cooed, examining the schedule on the desk in front of her. She leaned forward as she did it, and I thought, "The hell with it. I'll leap on her. What can they give me—20 years? It'll be worth it."

"Please take a seat," she murmured. "Doctor will be with you shortly."

The mad moment passed, and I was able to limp over to one of those chromium-and-leather chairs and collapse into it. There were two other patients waiting—both female, both beautiful and both looking like they had swallowed watermelons. Pregnant women remind me of past indiscretions, so I concentrated on Miss Bazooms behind the desk. It was either that or reading the current issue of *National Geographic*, and the Venus in the white uniform had it all over "Toads of the Lower Amazon."

Finally a buzzer buzzed, the receptionist smiled at me and said, "Doctor will see you now," and gestured toward a door leading into an inner office.

Bemott's private office looked like the Library of Congress. In fact, Dr. Warren G. Bemott looked like a young Senator, complete with lamp-tanned skin, silvery hair, a beautifully tailored grey flannel suit and a handshake just slightly firmer than a dead mackerel.

I went through the whole rigamarole once again, explaining who I was and what I was doing. He nodded patiently; apparently he had had experience talking to insurance investigators. He told me his story and it varied not one jot or tittle (that would make a great law firm—"Jot & Tittle") from his signed statement.

"Isn't it a little unusual that Mr. Baxter should lapse into a diabetic coma after taking his insulin so regularly?" I asked him.

He sighed heavily. "Very unusual. As a matter of fact, practically unheard of. Unless, of course, he had been extremely incautious about following his other instructions. For instance, if he had been drinking heavily or ingesting sugar in great amounts."

"And if he hadn't been taking the pills?"

"Oh, yes, in those circumstances a coma is quite understandable. But he *had* been taking his pills according to what Mag—according to what Mrs. Baxter and his daughter stated."

I nodded, showing no reaction to his slip. We chatted about the nature of diabetes for a few minutes, how it's incurable, how victims must take their insulin in pill form or by injection for the remainder of their lives, if they hoped to survive, and similar cheerful subjects.

"Thanks very much, doc," I said, and was gratified to see him wince when I called him "doc." I stood up to go. "Oh, by the way, do you also treat Magda Baxter and Terry Baxter?"

His face froze. "I fail to see what that has to do with your investigation."

"Just curious."

He thought a moment, I could almost hear the wheels turning.

"Terry Baxter is a patient of mine," he said finally. "Magda Baxter was on my list until about six months ago. At that time she expressed a desire to consult a gynecologist. I recommended a very good man in town, and she's been going to him ever since."

I nodded and started for the door. "Thanks very much, doc. Oh, by the way, can you tell me what these are?"

I spilled three pills from the dead man's pill bottle and held them out toward Bemott. He took one quick glance and looked me in the eye.

"Oral insulin," he said, and named the company who made them.

"How can you tell?"

"Shape of pill. Color. Size. Imprint of maker's initial on upper surface. There's no doubt."

"Thank you," I said, and then added, "doctor," for which he seemed properly grateful. On the way I stopped by the blonde receptionist's desk.

"The Waldorf-Astoria," I muttered to her. "Next Friday. At 9:30. Room 2467. You bring the rye bread."

"What?" she said. "What?"

I departed triumphantly, clouds of glory trailing behind me.

In the next two hours I did several things with such quick, military precision that General Davidson would have been proud of me. I had two extra-dry Beefeater martinis on-the-rocks (with a twist), a very rare sirloin and a heart-of-lettuce salad with oil-and-vinegar. I wrote my daily report and mailed it off to the Triple-I. I called the Baxter home and told the Brooklyn-accented maid that I'd like to buy her a drink. She giggled and said she couldn't possibly do it, and so we made a date to meet at a local cocktail joint that evening at 10:00. Meanwhile, on with the chase . . .

Robert Habbler, the pharmacist at the Garden Grove drugstore, was, I judged, about 32—but he could easily have passed for 48. He was grey-faced, tall, skinny, stoop-shouldered and there was something about his watery blue eyes that convinced me he was on something. It could have been coke, ludes or LSD—or maybe daily enemas. But it was *something*.

But when I mentioned Terry Baxter, a remarkable transformation took place. The poor slob straightened, his shoulders went back, his face got some color and he began to breathe heavily. Then I knew what he was hooked on.

I went through my routine and held out the pills.

"What are they?" I asked.

"Oral insulin," he said, just as Dr. Bemott had. And he also mentioned the maker's name.

"How do you know?"

"Size of pill. Shape. Color. Maker's initial on top."

"Do you make them up here?"

"Good heavens, no. We buy them in wholesale lots. Put them into little bottles when a prescription comes in."

"Could I buy them without a prescription?"

"Absolutely not," he said virtuously. "At least, not here."

I asked him if he'd contact Terry Baxter and tell her I'd be parked outside her house at midnight. He said he would, though he wasn't exactly delirious at the prospect.

I was beginning to see the pattern. It was there. A lot of little odds-and-ends of gossip, information, facts, lies. But it was all beginning to fall into place. I wanted to wind it up fast.

10:00 P.M.: Drinks with Irma Weber, the Brooklyn-accented maid of the Baxters. Expense account: $25.50 for five drinks for Irma (and five for me—all straight Jim Beam with water on the side). Results: Dr. Bemott had made a pass at Magda Baxter. She had repulsed him with indignation. And why not? Dr. Bemott might be good for $225,000 a year, but Jerome Baxter was worth over $8,000,000. Terry Baxter, the Lolita with golden fuzz on her tanned legs, had a crush on the handsome Dr Bemott. In turn, Robert Habbler, the grey-faced pharmacist, had a crush on Terry Baxter. The term "crush" as used here turned out to be an overwhelming sexual hang-up.

Irma was wearing a skirt considerably shorter than her maid's uniform, and it required the greatest mental discipline to get her back to the Baxter residence by midnight. As a matter of fact, I got her there by 11:15 and spent 45 minutes doing what she asked. I'm wicked—I know it, don't tell me—but it doesn't cost the Triple-I anything and it helped my cold. She wasn't wearing panties. I mention this in passing for readers interested in extraneous details. Oh yes, she had a small blue tattoo of a butterfly under her left breast. Interesting. I very rarely kiss a butterfly.

12:00 midnight: Terry Baxter came running out to the Pontiac, bosom heaving— you should excuse the expression. I had two questions for her:

(1) "Do you think Dr. Bemott is in love with your stepmother?"

"Of course not," she said indignantly. "But she's always making up to him, pressing herself against him, trying to make him. He tries to be very—you know—professional, but she's out of her mind about him."

(2) "How do you feel about your drugstore buddy, Robert Habbler?"

She sighed. "He's *infatuated* with me," she said finally, in the tones of a woman who has happily pinned another specimen to her display board, labeled: "My Favorite Victims."

I nodded. I was a long time silent. It was half facts and half me. I mean I couldn't back up what I *knew* had happened. I had no hard evidence. But the International Insurance Investigators pay me a helluva salary—and it's not all for hard evidence. They're buying my instincts.

"Okay," I said finally. "Here's how it happened. Your mother died—which hit you hard. Within two weeks your father remarried. You hate Magda. You considered killing her, but then thought better of it. You had a better idea. Or maybe Bobby Habbler had it. But I'll bet it was your idea. Your father had a $500,000 life insurance policy.

His wife was beneficiary. If he died from natural causes, she'd get it. Plus his share of the electronics company. A lot of loot. Are you listening?"

"Oh, yes," she said brightly. "I'm listening. It's very interesting."

"Okay," I went on, doing a lot of heavy thinking. "You don't give a damn for the druggist but you've really got the hots for Dr. Bemott. You are 16 and he's 38—but you're smart enough for a man of 132. The only rub here was that the doc was more interested in your stepmother than he was in you. Right?"

"She lured him," Terry Baxter said, "She tried to—"

"I know, I know," I interrupted. "His pitches got so embarrassing that she changed doctors. Sweetie, Magda was faithful to your father, no matter what you think. So let's go on: You're hot for Bemott. He's hot for Magda. Robert Habbler, the handy pharmacist, is hot for you. Add up all these hots and it comes out murder."

"Murder?" Terry gasped.

"Sure," I said, lighting a Pall Mall. "And I'll bet you never mentioned that horrid word to Habbler. But here's how you did it: You had your pet pharmacist make up some pills that looked exactly like the oral insulin. Any experienced pharmacist could do it. What did you pay, baby? Did you put out for him? Or did you just touch him up?"

"I just touched him up," she said in a low voice. "You're vulgar."

"And you're a killer," I nodded in the darkness of the Pontiac's front seat. "He probably used milk sugar or aspirin or chalk. But the pills looked great, and your father never knew the difference. Your *father*, baby. Are you listening?"

I sensed rather than saw the nod of her head.

"So you substituted the fake pills for the oral insulin in your father's pill box. You and your father and Magda go up to Vermont. He takes his useless pills and goes into a coma. His pill box disappears. You're figuring an investigation will be made, and you'll pin it on Magda. You still think she's taking Dr. Bemott away from you. You'll never believe she can't see him for dust."

"She's always—" she started.

"Forget it," I advised her. "Magda was faithful. You understand? *Faithful.* So you substitute the fake pills. The useless pills. So your father dies. Tough. But if Magda is convicted of his murder, all the dough will come to you. And *then* Dr. Bemott will be interested, because Dr. Bemott likes money —he likes it very much. Right, baby?"

"Yes," she sighed. "Right. But he's so beautiful . . ."

"The most beautiful man I've ever seen," I assured her solemnly. "And how are you going to make Magda the patsy? By planting that silver pill box with a few fake pills in her room, and then alerting me or the fuzz about it? I'll bet that box is in your room right now—isn't it, baby?"

She had the body of a 16-year-old and the mind of a sophisticated woman of 40.

"Can't we come to some arrangement?" she murmured.

It was like a military drill: thigh against thigh; fingers fumbling for my buttons; hot breath against my lips; wisps of long blonde hair tickling my cheek; slender fingers probing me, making me forget what had happened a short while ago with Irma Weber.

She was all over me like a wet sheet, grasping, clinging, panting, sweating. My God, she was 16 years old and had long, slender tanned legs covered with a golden down. Her body was new and relatively unused. Her breath was hot and sweet. In that crazy Pontiac we came together, and it was absolutely the greatest. I was breaking innumerable regulations, laws and moral codes—and didn't give a damn.

"That pill box," I breathed. "It's in your room—isn't it?"

"Oh yes," she murmured, "take me, take me!"

So I took her—that marvelous, golden, passionate, nutty 16-year-old. And afterwards, while she was still sleeping in the front seat of the Pontiac, I went up to her room and recovered Mr. Baxter's pill box with three completely useless sugar pills remaining.

I turned her in the next morning. They picked up Robert Habbler at the Garden Grove drugstore and sweated him for all of ten minutes before he confessed to everything I had known—or guessed.

So I got the Pontiac back to Manhattan, wrote up my report and stood at attention while General Davidson said, "Well done!"

Then, with two glorious days off. I went back to my pad and thought Deep Thoughts about life. Specifically, I thought of whom I might call to make pleasant my two unexpected days of leisure.

I thought of Magda Baxter, the soft, lush, easily bruised woman who had been faithful when it was so easy *not* to be faithful. I thought of her soft, sexy voice and her habit of coming up close to talk.

And I thought of Irma Weber, the Baxters' maid—solid, fun, a real swinger once you got enough drinks in her.

So, after all this heavy thought, I called Dr. Bemott's receptionist, the blonde in the white nylon uniform. She had one day off during the week and could come to Manhattan.

And she came!

The Ice Gang

The first time I saw her she was looking out through the broken glass in the side window of her father's jewelry store. She saw me looking at her, and gave me a half-smile before she pulled herself back inside. I thought she was the most beautiful woman I had ever seen.

I got a quick impression of dark, reddish hair, heavy eyebrows, lots of eye makeup, a pert, slender nose and a generous mouth, warm and inviting. There was a tiny black mole on her right cheek. I wanted to kiss it. All right . . . I'm a nut.

Her father was Herman Gessing, and he owned a jewelry store in Whipinig, Massachusetts, a small town about 20 miles north of Boston. Herman's store had been broken into three times within nine months. There were four other jewelry stores in Whipinig. Two of them had been taken twice, and the other two had one burglary apiece during the past year. The total swag taken was more than $900,000.

This was enough to alert the insurance company which covered all five stores in Whipinig. This was the Great Alabama Risk & Casualty Co., Inc.—a gem of a name for an insurance company that did all their business in New England. Great Alabama was about 100 years old and could easily stand the pinch, but they didn't like the idea of their five jewelry stores in one small Massachusetts town being taken like clockwork.

So Great Alabama called in the International Insurance Investigators—which is how I happened to get in on the fun-and-games. The Triple-I does claims investigations for a long list of clients—all insurance agencies— who, for one reason or another, are unable to make the frisk themselves. In this case, Great Alabama's Claims Department had three men on the sick list—one with a bullet through his gut—so they called us in. Our Boston office was up to its ears in a diamond smuggling case involving the port of Boston, so Lt. Gen. Lemuel K. Davidson, USMC (Ret.), the boss of the Triple-I, detached me from the Manhattan office and I headed north. Got all that straight?

So there she was—Hermione Gessing—
looking out the smashed window of her father's jewelry store in Whipinig, and I
thought she was beautiful. A few minutes
later I was inside the store, talking to her,
and I wanted to marry her—immediately.

Not only was she beautiful, but she was
strong. I mean you could see it. She was
wearing an off-the-shoulder peasant blouse,
and her shoulders and arms were tanned and
muscular. Her thighs were bulging the cloth
of her skirt, and every time she took a step
the calf muscle in her naked, shaved leg
moved in a way that made me swallow. She
had big, hard breasts; wide, firm hips; broad
shoulders; and she looked like she could toss
me over the left field fence any time she
wanted to. And I'd have loved it. Doctor,
tell me, what's wrong . . . ?

But what I had to do at the moment was
talk to her poppa, and she finally brought
Herman Gessing out of a back room. He was
an old, runty guy with eyeglasses that looked
like they were fitted with the bottoms of
Coke bottles. I flashed my potsy, explained
that I was doing the insurance investigation,
and I took him through his story of his three
robberies.

It wasn't very exciting. He had aluminum

foil strips around the edges of all his windows. You've seen the same strips outlining windows in hundreds of stores. Break the window and you break the strip. Break the strip and you set off an alarm in the local precinct house or in a private protective agency, depending on how the store is wired.

But Herman Gessing's jewelry store had been broken into three times and not once had the alarm gone off. That meant that either the switch had been turned off (it was located inside the store), or the thieves had figured some way to bridge the wire so they could break the window without calling in all the cops in Massachusetts.

I thanked Mr. Gessing, shook hands and said goodbye. I thanked Hermione Gessing, shook hands—and almost fainted. She had a grip that almost drove me to my knees. She was beautiful, and her smile was an invitation, but when she shook your hand, you felt sick. I mean this woman was *strong!*

I was booked into a motel a few miles outside of Whipinig. I filed the required daily report and sent it off to General Davidson. Then I ordered up a liter of my favorite plasma, Jim Beam, with ice cubes, soda and a reasonably clean glass. I constructed an excellent highball, kicked off my shoes, lay back on the bed, took a deep swallow and thought deeply about the case. And you know what I came up with? Nothing. Half a bottle later I fell asleep, gently and smoothly. And I woke up with the same result—nothing.

So I spent the next day visiting the other jewelry stores in Whipinig that had been taken. Like Gessing's, they all had that protective alarm system around their windows. And, like Gessing's, none of the alarm systems had worked during the burglaries. Three of the other four stores had male sales clerks. Big deal.

One store I visited was a place called Goodley's. The owner wasn't in, but the clerk who answered my questions was a guy named Steve McQuary. He looked like a surfer—six-feet-plus, tanned, handsome, white teeth and golden hair. Even before I smelled his cologne I suspected him.

But when he shook my hand, I almost passed out—again. The glittery lad had muscles and wanted to show them. I took him through the usual routine, and all I found out was what I already knew: Goodley's had been taken twice and both times the alarm system had failed to go off.

I moved across the street and sat in a drugstore phone booth and watched Goodley's doorway. Not many customers. Finally, shortly before noon, one guy went in and didn't come out, I figured maybe he was Mr. Goodley himself.

It was almost 12:30, and I was getting my share of dirty looks from the owner of the drugstore, when Steve McQuary came out of Goodley's and headed up Market Street, a jaunty plaid cap perched on his golden locks. I slid out of my phone booth, leaving five cigarette butts behind, and followed him, on the opposite side of the street. I figured it was his lunch hour, and he was heading home or heading for a restaurant. I was mildly bemused when he bought a ticket at the Whipinig Bijou, a movie theatre, and went inside.

Well, a clerk in a jewelry store could go to a movie on his lunch hour; there was no law against it. In fact, it made sense; the Bijou was showing old Chaplin comedies.

I went inside, and locating McQuary was no chore; there were only about 20 people in the whole theatre. He was in the back row, far over on one side, and even in the dimness I could see he was sitting next to a broad.

Then I got close enough to see who she

was, and I thought, "Hermione, you've not been faithful to me!"

It was Hemione Gessing, all right, and she was muttering away at a fast clip to McQuary. She also passed him an envelope. As I watched, he took out the contents of the envelope, tucked them into the breast pocket of his jacket, crumpled the envelope and let it drop on the theatre floor.

They sat together for about ten minutes, then Hermione split. I made sure she didn't spot me. After another ten minutes, Mc-Quary departed. Curiouser and curiouser. I debated with myself which one I should tag, and then decided neither. My bet was that they were both going back to their respective stores.

So I waited a few moments after McQuary left, then went over to the seats the two had occupied. I retrieved the crumpled envelope McQuary had dropped and stuffed it into my pocket.

Then I went out, found a fine German restaurant and had an enormous plate of knockwurst and sauerkraut and baked beans, all washed down with two steins of dark. Great. I waited until I was on my second cup of coffee before I took the crumpled envelope out of my pocket and smoothed it out.

It wasn't much help, It was a white business envelope with Herman Gessing's name and address printed in the upper left-hand corner. I turned it over and over. The light in the restaurant was bad, but I thought I saw the imprint of something on the back, as if someone had written something on a paper that was over the envelope, and the point of the pencil had gone through and made a vague imprint.

I took the envelope back to my hotel room and put a strong light on it, tilting a desk lamp so the glare hit at an angle across the faint imprint. I stared at it, tilting the envelope this way and that, and eventually I made a guess and jotted it all down. It said "K-5, S-10, B-5, L-4."

"Elementary, my dear Watson," I said aloud, taking out my almost depleted bottle of Beam and buying myself a drink, "this is obviously a code for an opening chess move that is impossible to defeat."

"K-5, S-10, B-5, L4." What the hell? The more I puzzled over it, the less sense it made. So, like the idiot I am, I called Hermione Gessing and asked her for a date. I asked her if she'd have dinner with me and maybe see a movie or go dancing or whatever she wanted.

I think I shook her up—which was one of the reasons I called. But, after about ten seconds of silence, she recovered quickly and said she'd be delighted. She almost gushed. I made arrangements to pick her up at her daddy's store at 6:00 P.M.

At this stage of the game I was playing it strictly by ear. I had no great plan I'm not telling you about, and I had no very clear idea of what was going on in Whipinig. But I suspected—and I imagine you do, too—that someone in one of the five Whipinig jewelry stores was involved in the burglaries. That business of the alarms not going off was the sticking point. It sounded to me like someone who knew about the alarms was turning them off, robbing the premises by coming through the door, and then smashing the windows on the way out to make it look like an ordinary Breaking & Entering. Or maybe—and this was, I admit, a wild hunch —maybe the stores were being looted during the day, and the smashed windows were just a coverup.

The more I thought about it, the less wild it sounded. Suppose a clerk in a jewelry store—someone like Hermione Gessing or Steve McQuary—systematically takes a few hunks of ice every day—rings, bracelets, watches, small stuff they can take out with no trouble. Then, when they think the owner might get suspicious or maybe when an inventory is coming up, they stage a fake burglary to cover the theft.

It sounded good as a one-man operation but, I kept telling myself, all five Whipinig jewelry stores had been hit. So I stopped thinking, showered, changed and went to pick up Hermione Gessing.

She was wearing something thin, floating, gossamer. It was wide as a tent, came high on her neck and had long sleeves. It also seemed to end a few inches below her waist.

"The customers must love you," I said to her.

She laughed, and confessed she had gone home to change late in the afternoon.

God, her legs were great, Tanned, smooth, absolutely hairless, with slender ankles, a plump bulge of calf, little dimples behind her knees, and then the long, hard muscles of her thighs rippling under the skin. I'd have been willing to spend the evening right there, staring at her legs, but I figured I had to feed the chick, so we took off.

She knew of a roadhouse a few miles outside of town which, she claimed, served great steaks and also had a small combo that provided music for dancing after dinner. That sounded good to me. I figured I'd need a steak if I was going to push this strong dame around the dance floor.

It turned out to be a very pleasant evening indeed. The steaks weren't all that great, but they were edible, and the drinks were generous. I had no trouble getting her to talk; as a matter of fact, about the only time she closed her mouth was when there was a hunk of steak in it.

We didn't talk about the burglaries, but I asked her how she kept in such good physical condition, and she said she worked out three evenings a week at a very popular health club in Whipinig that offered classes in modern dance and ballet, karate and judo, had handball and badminton courts, and stuff like that. Hermione was a gymnast, working on the horse, rings and parallel bars.

I watched her as she talked, her eyes glinting in the light from the candle on the table, and I could see that she was a physical culture nut, telling me how important it was to have a "sound body." She had a sound body, all right . . . a beautiful sound. And the face wasn't bad either. Except, maybe, it was just a little too strong, a little too firm and determined. But I wasn't about to quibble over trifles.

We were finishing our brandy when the combo came on, and we got up to dance. It was strictly Lawrence Welk, but that was okay with me. I was beginning to feel the bourbon, the wine and the brandies, and I needed something slow and easy while I recovered my strength.

She came into my arms like a dream. She was light on her feet, and she fitted herself to me like a silk glove. The lights were dimmed, and her hand on my back crept up until it was resting on the nape of my neck. Her head went down on my shoulder, and wisps of that thick, reddish hair tickled my nose. She was wearing a gardenia scent, which always turns me on, and occasionally I could feel her warm breath on my cheek.

But what really drove me through the top of my skull was that firm, soft, hot, cool, strong, whippy body pressed against me. My hand was pressed in the middle of her back, and I felt around casually a few moments.

"No," she murmured. "No bra."

I didn't think so. And then also casually—really not caring, you understand—the Lannihan paw fell to her waist, and a bit lower to the beginning of her hips. I could feel no elastic or panty top through the thin cloth of her dress.

"No," she murmured, as we moved slowly around the darkened dance floor, "nothing there either."

I mean this dame was thoroughly and completely naked under that thin, floating tent of silk she wore. What a nut! But why complain? I pulled her a little tighter, and she didn't resist at all. I looked around nervously, and no one seemed to be observing us. As a matter of fact, there were four other couples on the floor doing exactly what we were doing. And one couple seemed to be performing vertically what is usually accomplished horizontally.

Hermione sighed and leaned closer into me, her breasts wilting my shirt, her strong pelvis coming at me with a little grind. One hand was caressing the back of my neck; our clasped hands were bent close to our shoulders and she was tickling my palm. She sighed. I sighed.

Occasionally I led her back to our table, limping, and we had a glass of champagne. Then she'd lead me back onto the floor again, and plaster her warmth against me, and we'd start with the sighs again.

Around midnight I started making sounds

like maybe I should get her home. She stalled me and stalled me but finally, a little after 1:00 A.M., I got her out of the place and drove her home. We were both somewhat high—on booze and the dancing and the heat of the roadhouse. But I also had a strange feeling that she was acting a little drunker than she was. She was doing a stage routine of how a drunk acts, lurching too much, slurring the wrong words, her head wobbling as she grinned inanely.

We pulled up in front of her house. There was one dim bulb burning on the front porch. I killed my lights and cut the engine. I started to tell her, formally, how much I enjoyed the evening. I thanked her, and I wished . . . and then you know what that crazy dame did?

"Look," she said with a feline grin, and she lifted that voluminous tent-dress up off her body until it was wrapped around her arms, shoulders and head. There she sat, wearing shoes, a dress wrapped around her head . . . and nothing else. I put on the dash light. You think I'm a fool?

You wouldn't believe it. She had an all-over tan—I mean *all* over—and that incredible strong, rippling, muscular body moved slowly around with a rhythm all its own.

"Lannihan," I said to myself bitterly, "you're a fool."

So I got into the back seat with her and she showed me just how talented and inventive a lady-type gymnast can be. Talk about pretzels! If I'd had a video camera with me, I could have become the new Porn King.

About an hour later I got her inside her house, clothed, and I went home to my motel and fell thankfully into bed, snoring almost immediately.

And if you want to know why I called myself a fool back there in the car, when she was rubbing around beside me, it was because I knew damned well she was stalling me. She wanted to be with me just as long as she could. And sure enough, at about 10:30 A.M. the next morning, I was awakened by a phone call from Chief Braisley of the Whipinig Police Department. He thought I might be interested to know that around 2:00 A.M. that morning, Lopez & Jones—another of Whipinig's five jewelry stores—had been broken into. The take was about 30 G's.

So much for love and romance. Wolf Lannihan, the Demon Detective—always on the job.

I got over there a little after noon, and Ben Jones, the son of one of the owners, answered my questions. He was one of the two clerks in the store, opened up every morning and laid out the stock. But this morning Braisley had called him about 4:00 A.M. when the cops on the beat discovered the smashed window and looted shelves. I nodded dismally. I headed for the nearest tavern. I wasn't feeling so hot.

After a double Beam on-the-rocks, I began to feel the plasma take hold, and the old nerve ends began to tingle again. I flipped out a cigarette and reached in my side pocket for my lighter. I came out with the slip of paper on which I had written "K-5, S-10, B-5, L-4," the writing I had deciphered from that envelope Steve McQuary had discarded on the floor of the Bijou Theatre, the day he met Hermione Gessing.

Idly, I added up the numbers. They came to 24. I had been thinking about the 30 G's just lifted from Lopez & Jones, and the number 24 interested me. Suppose the letters and numbers indicated people and what their share of the take would be. Let's see now . . . "S" could be Steve McQuary, the clerk at Goodley's. And "B" could be Ben Jones, the clerk at Lopez & Jones. Hmm, I left my new hooker of Mr. Beam long enough to make two phone calls. Everything came up roses.

The clerk at Harvester Jewelry was a chick, Katherine Bradley. She could be "K." And the clerk at Everfine Jewelry Company was Lloyd Holtzer. He could be "L." My, my.

Now suppose there was a fifth member of this little group, and her notation read H-6. That would be dear, sweet, soft, strong, sexy Hermione Gessing, and her share of the Lopez & Jones take would be six thousand. And why would the "S"—standing for Steve McQuary—get more than the others? Maybe because, on this particular job, he did the actual breaking and entering, and thus took the most risk. "Lannihan, m'lad," I muttered half-aloud, "you're a genius."

"Another one?" the wizened bartender asked.

"Nope, not for me. Have one yourself."

"Never touch the stuff," he said. "It rusts your pipes."

So? Who wants shiny pipes?

There was one more thing I wanted to do before I blew the whistle. That evening I paid a visit to the Frankenheimer Health Club, the gym where Hermione Gessing gave her incredible body tri-weekly workouts.

It was a surprisingly well-equipped, clean

and efficiently operated place—if you don't mind the smell of honest sweat. They had a small pool in the basement, sauna and Turkish bath, handball and badminton courts, a room devoted to grunting weightlifters, a large general gym with the usual wall bars, parallel bars, leather horses, rings and a trapeze.

I told the old man on duty at the front desk that I was staying in Whipinig a few weeks, wanted to keep in trim and would like to look around. He waved me upstairs and said, "Help yourself."

I spotted Ben Jones in the weightlifters' room, trying to jerk-and-press more weight than he could handle. Nice build on the kid. Steve McQuary was on the mat in the karate class, shouting, "Hah! Uhh! Kah!" as he slashed with the edge of his hand at a small Japanese who wasn't making a sound but who wasn't getting hit, either.

Up in the large gym, there was my dream girl, Hermione, wearing a bright purple leotard and doing things on the parallel bars you wouldn't believe possible unless you saw it. Her body was a blur of movement as she went through a constant flow of twirls, handstands, splits, reverse falls, etc. Her face, arms and legs were slick with sweat, but she looked great.

"Too bad, baby," I thought sadly, and remembered how crazy and wonderful she had looked sitting beside me in the car, her dress tossed over her head, her naked body gleaming dully in the dash light.

Chief Braisley and the Whipinig cops had a small department and could only provide two night stakeouts. I brought in two free-lancers from a Boston private-eye outfit we had worked with before. I was the fifth man. We put stake-outs on the five jewelry stores. Naturally, I cleared all these arrangements with boss man Davidson in Manhattan. I figured it might take a month before the Wet Armpits Gang struck again, and I wanted the General to okay the expense.

Actually, it took a little less than three weeks. Then they hit Harvester Jewelry for the second time, Ben Jones doing the actual B&E. He was wearing a black leather jacket, black turtleneck sweater, black jeans, socks and shoes.

I was down the block, crouched in the back seat of my arthritic Pontiac. I watched him go in the door with a key (no alarm went off), heard the sounds of the smashing of display cases and then saw him come out and toss a padded brick through the front window. The whole thing took about ten minutes and made less noise than you might expect. It was 3:00 in the morning, and there wasn't a soul on the street. Except me.

When Ben turned around, after demolishing the front window of Harvester, I was standing there, my hands in my pockets.

"Hi, Ben," I said cheerily.

He didn't hesitate a second. He fell into the classic karate stance, feet spread, arms out in front of him, palms held at an angle, fingers together. He shuffled toward me.

"Hah!" he shouted.

"Hah, yourself," I said genially, took one hand out of my pocket and shot the legs out from under him.

It took a few weeks to wrap it up. As usual, the men blabbered, and the two women wouldn't say a word. They had all been looting their respective stores, and then covering up with amateurish smash-and-grab raids late at night. They had known each other vaguely, all being in the same business, but their real link was the body-building angle. The three men were karate students and weightlifters. The two women were gymnasts. After every workout at Frankenheimer's, they had diet cola together and planned their next caper.

If they had any leader it was Hermione Gessing, although it came out at the trial that Steve McQuary did most of the strong-arm work and got a larger share of the loot. But Hermione did the planning, made out the schedules, sold the ice to Boston fences and decided how much each of the five would receive. They never questioned her decisions. Like I said—a strong woman.

I only saw her once after that. They all got five-to-ten, and they were bringing them out of the courtroom. She passed close to me, looked up and stared into my eyes.

"As a dancer, you're lousy," she said.

"But on the back seat of a five-year-old Pontiac?" I asked her.

She smiled.

An Introduction to Murder

When I started as a gumshoe with the International Insurance Investigators about six zillion years ago, the boss man of the outfit was Mac Brady. I guess I've already told you how he caught it in a shoot-out with three South American revolutionaries who had just hijacked a Brazil-bound shipment of gold bars.

Anyway, Mac Brady was a short, dumpy, rumple-faced guy with an angry way of talking. I hated him on sight. After he was killed, I cried for three days and finally realized how much he meant to me. Of course, it was too late to tell him. That's the way those things go.

I had been two years with Army CID, and I had a letter to Brady from the CO of my outfit. Brady read the letter, looked over my record and nodded.

"Okay," he said. "You're hired."

274

"What?" I said.

"You're hired, That's what you came in here for, wasn't it?"

"Oh . . . yeah . . . sure," I stammered. "But I should tell you, Mr. Brady, that I don't know much about the insurance business."

"Who does?"

"I mean, most of my cases overseas were rape, theft of government property, assaulting an officer—stuff like that. I've never handled a murder case, for instance."

"Oh shut up and get to work," he growled. He slid a file across the desk with sufficient force so that it slid off and landed neatly in my lap. "A rich-type guy knocked himself off up on East 82nd Street two nights ago. A .22 pistol shot through the right temple. He was covered by Arcana Insurance. They're one of our clients. The nick is 400 G's. Arcana Claims Department is jammed up and wants us to check it out. Got all that?"

"I don't know what the hell you're talking about," I told him.

He pulled his lips apart in a kind of grin.

"You'll learn," he said. "It's all in the file. Don't forget to submit daily written reports. Now beat it."

"Yes, *sir!*" I said.

"The name's Mac," he yelled as I went out the door.

It was my first case with the Triple-I, and I knew damned well if I muffed it, Mac Brady would tie a can to my tail as fast as he had hired me. He was that kind of guy.

I went back down to Personnel, told them I had been hired and asked for a desk. They put me in something that looked like a converted broom closet. Converted but not enlarged. I opened the file Mac Brady had tossed at me and started reading.

Richard Holmes . . . 48 . . . married two years before . . . no children . . . Occupation: Investor . . . Widow: Corinne Holmes (formerly Corinne LaFrance, 28) . . . lived with his wife and his sister, Evelyn . . . two servants: houseman and cook . . . Mr. and Mrs. James Rafferty, inhabiting basement apartment of the Holmes townhouse . . . found shortly after midnight sprawled on the rug of his second-floor library . . . single .22 shot through right temple . . . death probably instantaneous . . . gun near right hand . . . prints of deceased on gun . . . no note . . . no record of previous suicide tries . . . police verdict: Suicide . . . gun unregistered . . . body found by wife . . . deceased in good financial condition . . . insured with

Arcana Insurance, Inc. for $400,000 . . . beneficiary: Wife . . .

I slapped the file shut and looked up in the air. "Now what do I do?" I asked aloud.

What I did was look up Holmes, Richard, on East 82nd Street, in the Manhattan telephone directory and put a call through. I got a whiskey tenor right out of County Cork. James Rafferty, no doubt. I asked for the widow, Corinne Holmes. He said she was out making funeral arrangements for "himself." I asked for the sister, Evelyn Holmes, and explained who I was. He put me through.

A low-pitched voice, a bit husky, but under control. I went through the identification bit again and asked for an appointment.

"Tomorrow afternoon at 3:30," she said. "The funeral will be over then."

"Thank you," I said humbly. "Would you mention to Mrs. Holmes that I'll be there tomorrow and would like to talk to her as well, if it's convenient."

"I shall inform Mrs. Holmes," she said acidly, coming down hard on the "Mrs."

I spent the rest of the day getting my Triple-I ID card and drawing a .38 S&W Police Special from the Armory. I banged away in the basement range for almost an hour and was satisfied. It tossed up a bit and to the right, but as long as I knew about it, I didn't care.

It was a fine old greystone townhouse in a very fashionable neighborhood indeed. The guy who let me in, James Rafferty himself, was wearing a shiny black suit. He was also wearing the biggest, reddest nose I've seen since W. C. Fields passed on to the Jugglers' Heaven. A lot of good booze had gone into the making of that nose, and from the way Rafferty was slurring his consonants and occasionally propping himself against a wall as he showed me upstairs, I figured the funeral of his employer had been a good excuse for him to try a wee nip of the old nasty.

Evelyn Holmes, the sister, was waiting for me in the library—the room where the corpse had been found, I recalled from the file. She sat behind a leather-topped desk and made no effort to get up or greet me or shake hands. But she did ask me to sit down. That was nice of her.

About 38, I guessed. Black hair parted in the middle, drawn down severely across her brow and then flaring up into curled wings over her ears. She might have worn black at the funeral, but right now she was wearing a scoop-necked white dress with lace and a drawstring at top. Very sexy. There was a

Victorian desk lamp, lighted, almost in front of her. It hid part of her face. The window drapes were drawn. The desk lamp was the only illumination in the room.

Full lips . . . beautiful complexion . . . very composed . . . no expression . . . elbows on desk, chin propped on the backs of her folded hands . . . grave grey eyes . . . a steady, unblinking stare from those eyes . . . but I had a hard time keeping my eyes off those bare shoulders . . . the flesh . . . a hint of cleavage between her breasts . . . had she planned it that way?

"How can I help you, Mr. Lannihan?" the low, husky, completely controlled voice asked.

This wasn't some poor, liquored-up GI who had slugged his captain in a moment of uncontrollable fury. I had to walk softly here. I explained that my investigation was purely routine, that we had the official police report of her brother's death, that I was asking questions only to fill in a few small gaps in the overall picture.

She pushed the leather swivel chair back from the desk and reached for a pack of cigarettes.

"Ask away," she nodded.

I leaned over the desk to hold my Zippo

for her and got a look at her legs. Great. No stockings. Smooth and tanned. The short white skirt was hiked up, and she made no schoolgirlish effort to tug it down. How to seduce a detective.

I took her over her activities on the night her brother's body was found. There was little she could add to what I had already read in the police report . . .

She had had dinner with her brother and sister-in-law in the first-floor dining room, a meal prepared by Martha Rafferty and served by James.

"Does he drink?" I asked.

"Oh yes," she said.

After coffee and brandy, Corinne Holmes departed for a rehearsal of *Skylark* by her theatre group. Apparently she was very active in the group and appeared in its plays.

"Before my brother married her," Evelyn said in a peculiarly corrosive voice, "my sister-in-law had theatrical ambitions."

So Corinne departed for her rehearsal. Richard Holmes came upstairs to the library where we were presently seated to work on his tax returns. Evelyn went on up to the third floor where she had a two-room suite, bedroom and sitting room, to watch a television show she wanted to see. The show ended at 11:00 and she decided to take the family pet, an Afghan, for a walk along the river. She was gone for almost an hour.

"Aren't you worried, walking your dog at that hour on New York streets?" I asked her.

"Of course not," she said, wide-eyed, seemingly amazed at the idiocy of anyone questioning her courage.

She returned from her walk and then there was a scene of pure chaos. Her brother had killed himself. His wife had returned from her rehearsal and found the body. Martha Rafferty had awakened from a sound sleep and promptly became hysterical. James Rafferty was drunk. The cops were called. It was quite a night.

"I understand it was an unregistered gun," I said, making a pretext of looking down at my notebook. "How long had your brother had it?"

"It wasn't *his* gun," she said immediately. "It was Corinne's. She was in a play about a year ago in which one of the actors is supposedly killed on stage. Blanks, of course. Corinne bought the gun and then, when the play ended, she brought it home."

"So you know where she bought it?"

"No."

"Do you know where she kept it?"

"In their bedroom, I suppose."

"Did you know if they had bullets for it? Real bullets, not blanks?"

"I didn't know that, no. I never saw it after she brought it home."

"Could your brother have kept it in his desk?"

"He could have."

"Could your brother or sister-in-law have purchased bullets for it?"

"They could have, yes."

"Did your brother keep large amounts of cash on the premises?"

"Not to my knowledge. We paid everything by check. We have a wall safe behind that copy of a Renoir, over there, but there's nothing in it but passports and nonnegotiable securities, my brother's will . . . things like that."

"Do you know who the beneficiaries are to his estate?"

"He told me. Two-thirds to Corinne. The remaining third to me, the Rafferty couple, his college, and a few other minor bequests. You understand, of course, that I am independently wealthy through a bequest from our parents."

"Of course," I nodded, though I had

known nothing of the sort. I stood up, snapped my notebook shut and smiled at her. "Would it be possible to see Mrs. Holmes now?" I asked.

"She's in her sitting room. One flight up, first door on the right at the head of the stairs. She's waiting for you."

"Thank you. Then I'd like to speak to James and Martha Rafferty for a few moments, if I may."

"Naturally,"

She stood up, finally, and I was surprised to see what a tall woman she was. She moved slowly, deliberately and with grace. She showed me to the door and I thought she stood too close to me, but it could have been my imagination. I put my hand on the doorknob, paused, then turned to her as if with an afterthought.

"Oh, by the way, Miss Holmes," I said, "what are your relations with your sister-in-law?"

She looked at me; our eyeballs locked. Something came into hers—a steely strength.

"Cordial, Mr. Lannihan," she said calmly. "Quite cordial."

I got out of there. Questioning that dame was a lot different from putting the screws on a hungover Pfc.

The widow, Corinne Holmes, was something else again. Small, blonde (obviously dyed), sharp-featured, wearing a thin, black silk shift that did little to cover the electric intensity in her flat-breasted, thin-shanked figure. Her hands fluttered like birds—patting her hair, lighting a cigarette, smoothing her dress, plucking at the arm of her chair—they didn't stop a moment.

And her voice was pure theatre: resonant, projecting, with careful enunciation.

Yes, they had had dinner and then she had gone to her rehearsal, She returned shortly after midnight. Not finding her husband in their suite on the third floor, she had come down to the library and found his body. She supposed she screamed. James Rafferty came running up from the basement. He was quite drunk but operating well enough to call the cops.

I asked her about the gun.

It had been purchased during a motor trip to Texas the Holmeses had made almost 18 months ago. She knew her theatre group planned a production of a play that required a pistol shot on stage. She bought the gun in a state where, at the time, weapons were sold in almost every hardware, drug and variety store—no questions asked. She bought a box of blank cartridges at the same time. She had never purchased actual bullets for the gun. As far as she knew, her late husband had never bought any. The gun was kept in the lower drawer of a dresser they shared in the master bedroom.

I listened to that marvelous voice and watched the nervous, twitching woman who apparently was held together with piano wire. I threw a hard one at her.

"Silly question, Mrs. Holmes," I said, 'but did you love your husband?"

She didn't hesitate a second.

"He was the best thing that ever happened to me," she gasped. "I was on the fringes of the theatre. I knew I'd never make it. I was getting older . . . older. I had walk-ons and bit parts. Cheap, furnished apartment. Making the rounds. Lousy food. I had failed, and I knew it. You understand? He rescued me from all that."

"I understand," I nodded. "But you still haven't answered my question. Did you love him?"

"Love him?" she groaned, and the back of her hand went to her forehead in a gesture so theatrical that I almost smiled. "No, I don't suppose I did. Can an actress love anyone except herself? But he was the dearest, sweetest, kindest man who ever lived, and I'd have cut my throat before doing anything that would hurt him."

"How do you feel about your sister-in-law?"

"That bitch? I could cut *her* throat and get the best night's sleep in my life!"

I got nothing out of Martha Rafferty except substantiation of what Evelyn and Corinne had told me. When it came to the red-nosed James, I suggested we might step around the corner to a pub I had noticed and discuss the whole thing over a convivial glass.

"A splendid suggestion, sir." He beamed. "I shall be delighted to accompany you."

So there we were, happily tucked into a back booth of The Crazy Unicorn, one of those imitation English pubs that are springing up all over Manhattan.

"What's your pleasure, Mr. Rafferty?" I asked.

"Whatever you might mention, sir," he said amiably.

Before he got too bombed, I took him over the events of the death night. I learned nothing new except that the widow had a case of the weeps, and the sister never shed a tear.

"A cold one, that scut," Rafferty said sourly.

Then I got him onto something that had puzzled and intrigued me for more than 24 hours: the personality and character of the dead man. Just what kind of a guy was he?

"The pore man, the pore man," Rafferty mourned. "Driven by women all his life, he was. First his mother—God rest the old bitch's soul—and then by his sister. A quiet, calm, meek, sad, accommodating man, he was. Do anything you asked him to. No spine, you understand, but sweet and colorless he was. Driven by women. Another?"

"Of course," I said, motioning the waiter.

"And then he met and married Miss Corinne," Rafferty went on, his eyeballs getting a bit glazed now. "A thin, nervy woman as she is. No meat to her . . . but a woman for all that. So he married her and I saw him smile and laugh. Him who had never smiled or laughed in his life before. Enough to make a strong man weep."

And he began to weep. I looked around nervously to make sure no one was staring at us, then shoved his drink closer to him. He took a deep gulp and the tears stopped as if they had been turned off by an automatic valve.

"And him so sick," he said.

"Sick?" I asked. "Richard Holmes was sick?"

"Sick," Rafferty nodded, "and dying in the bargain. Told me so himself. Swore me to secrecy. Here . . ." And then he thumped himself on his great barrel chest. "The poor, shriveled heart of the man," he went on mournfully. "Could go like that . . ." and he tried to snap his fingers.

"You took him to the doctor?" I prodded.

"Twice a week," he said, nodding. "Gustafson, Medical Building. On 60th Street, between Park and Lex. Best man in the country, he told me. But no hope. No hope for poor Richard Brinsley Holmes. I drink to him!" he shouted suddenly, rising to his feet and weaving back and forth. "And I'll kill any man who won't!"

So I rose to my feet and drank to Richard Brinsley Holmes and got a lot of cold stares from the other customers and a disapproving shake of the head from the bartender.

Just before he became completely unintelligible, I asked James Rafferty what he wanted to do, what his dreams and ambitions were. It was that kind of moment.

"Dublin," he murmured. "Back to Dublin . . . can do it now . . . got the green . . .

Dublin . . . that bitch . . . the poor sod, the poor sod . . . driven by women he was . . . ah, the darkness . . ."

I liked him and got him home and into his basement apartment before he passed out. I hoped he'd make it to Dublin.

I went back to my ratty hotel room—the one I took as temporary quarters before I applied for the job at the Triple-I. (I've been living there now for 11 years.)

I called Records at headquarters and asked the duty man to run a check on any savings or checking account of James Rafferty.

I called Dr. Gustafson on East 60th Street. He wasn't in. I explained to his receptionist that it was extremely urgent that I see the doctor for just a few minutes in the morning. She said I could come in at 10:15 A.M., precisely. I thanked her humbly.

I called the precinct house that had answered the call the night Richard Holmes died, and finally got hold of the detective who was saddled with the case. I identified myself, and he said to give him my number, hang up and he'd call me back.

So he checked me out and called back in about ten minutes. He wasn't overjoyed to talk about the case on the telephone, but he finally told me what I wanted to know:

Richard Holmes' fingerprints came up loud and clear on the pistol found near his right hand. There were no other prints on the gun.

"Isn't that a little unusual?" I asked him. "The wife claims it was her pistol, that it was used in a play she was in. Her prints should be there. Maybe other actors'. That pistol should have been a smear of prints, all loused up."

There was silence for almost a minute.

"Yeah, it's freaky," he sighed finally. "I thought the same thing myself. But the verdict was suicide. I got 18 other cases I'm running right now. What do you want me to do?"

"I'm sorry," I said, and I really meant it. "I didn't mean to bug you. If anything comes up, I'll be in touch."

"You do that," he said heavily, and hung up.

My last call of the day was to Evelyn Holmes. I asked her if I might meet with her the next day, around noon. She said I could come over at 12:30, and I thanked her.

I didn't feel like eating. I felt like drinking and thinking. I broke out a new pint of Jim Beam and chipped some ice cubes loose from that safe the hotel management called a refrigerator. I put the cubes in a fogged toothbrush glass and doused them with the good bourbon. I kicked off my shoes, flopped down on the mortuary slab they called a bed, took a deep belt and started thinking . . .

Don't let anyone kid you—in the business of crime detection, on any level—local, state, federal, international—a good detective depends mostly on his experience, his instinct and guesses. This stuff about "logical detection" is for the birds. It all depends on how much you know about people, their motives, what moves them and what you'd do if you were in their spot.

So there I was, drinking and guessing, when the phone rang. It was the duty man in Records at Triple-I. He reported that James Rafferty had been putting $60 a month in his savings account for several years. About a year ago, his deposit jumped to $100 a month. Two days ago, James Rafferty had deposited $18,000 in cash. They had been unable to check the source of this sudden wealth.

I thanked him, hung up, had a final belt of Mr. Beam and went to sleep. I had a dream about Evelyn Holmes, the details of which are none of your business.

My morning meeting with Dr. Gustafson only took about five minutes, but he told me what I wanted to know. He was an old geezer with bags under his eyes hanging halfway down his cheeks. He looked like he'd check out a lot sooner than most of the patients sitting nervously in his waiting room.

"Oh yes," he sighed, "I read about Richard Holmes' suicide in the *Times*. Understandable. He developed this cardiac condition about a year ago. I'd explain it to you, but you wouldn't understand it. He could have gone any moment. Any moment of any day. So the suicide didn't disturb me. It was his decision."

"One thing, doctor," I asked him. "If there was an autopsy, would it show if he had died of cardiac failure before the bullet was fired?"

He stared at me a long time. This old doctor had seen everything. Nothing could rock him.

"Yes," he said finally, "an autopsy would show that."

"Thank you, doctor," I said briskly, and left.

This time Martha Rafferty answered the door; I suppose James was still sleeping off his hangover. And this time I was shown to

Evelyn Holmes' suite on the third floor. Pleasant sitting room, bedroom and bathroom. Apparently she was an amateur artist; there was a taboret, paint-smeared palette, a small canvas, brushes (handles down) in a glass jar. There was a bowl of fresh fruit on her desk top; she had been trying to capture their live colors.

She was wearing an orange smock, a loose thing that was buttoned up to her neck and fell in long folds about her bare legs. She was wearing sandals. I loved her toes.

When she showed me in, she was sipping from a glass of wine, and the open bottle of burgundy—a gallon jug—was resting on the floor. I accepted her invitation and had a glass. I'm the kind of nut who prefers red wine chilled, but I didn't tell her that. I drank her room-temperature burgundy and liked it.

"What can I do for you, Mr. Lannihan?" she asked lazily, standing in front of the easel, brushing in a few strokes, then looking at the bowl of fruit.

"Where did you buy the bullets for the gun?" I asked her.

"I never bought bullets for any gun," she said, still painting away.

"All right," I sighed. "So we'll check your

293

movements and find out what other states you've visited in the last year. We'll keep prying and probing and nosing, and eventually we'll find out where you bought them. Is that enough?"

She put the brush down, wiped her hands on a rag, slowly walked over to the door and locked it. Then she came toward me, staring at me, eyes locked, deliberately unbuttoning the silly orange smock.

You know, she wasn't wearing a stitch underneath—not a stitch. And her body was good, damned good. I had a confused impression of smooth, tanned skin, everything rose-tipped, curves and shadows, gleaming warmth. Then her arms were about me and she was pressing close. It was like being pushed up against a furnace.

"Not money," she said. "Because you'd want more and more and more. But maybe we can come to some other arrangements . . ."

Like I told you, it was my first case—so I pushed her away. But my hands remained on the hot flare of her naked hips. I wanted to feel her.

"No," I said, and I didn't recognize my own voice. "No deal."

"No one else thinks I killed him," she

said, and her voice was strange and strangled in her throat.

So I was a weak bastard and pulled her close and ran my fingernails up and down her naked back, stroking her into a kind of throbbing frenzy.

"Why, baby," I whispered in her ear, "you didn't kill him. Because you're a great, big, strong woman, but you can't kill. You'd be surprised how few people can—in cold blood. You came down to the library for some reason or other. And you found him dead. This was after you brought the dog back from his evening walk. Your brother died from a heart attack. It could have happened any minute in the last year. But you didn't know that. You only knew he was dead. And that hate you had for your sister-in-law started working . . ."

"Yes," she gasped, naked body trembling, "yes . . ."

"You had bought the bullets," I went on, "just from some nutty idea of having a loaded weapon in the house, maybe thinking that some day you'd kill—not him but *her*."

"God, yes," she moaned. "I would have shot her—eventually!"

"Sure," I said, still stroking that warm, smooth back. "But this was better. Your brother died from natural causes. A chance to pin it on his wife—a woman you hated. How were you going to do it?"

"The bullets," she muttered in my ear. "I gave her name, left her card. They'd think she bought them."

"Oh, sure," I told her, not wanting to mention how stupid she had been. "So you found your brother dead, went back upstairs, got the pistol from their dresser, loaded it, came back down, put a bullet through his dead brain, wiped the pistol clean, then carefully clamped the pistol in his hand and then let it fall. But all of a sudden, sooner than you expected, there was old drunken James Rafferty brought up from his basement apartment by the sound of the shot. And you looked up and there he was. And you gave him 18 big ones to keep his mouth shut. How am I guessing?"

"Oh, God, God . . ." she moaned. "How many years will I get?"

"With your dough and your influence?" I said, "you probably won't get a long afternoon. There will have to be an autopsy, of course, but if your brother really died of natural causes, they'll probably sweep the whole thing out the window."

"Thank you," she murmured, "Thank you . . ."

She pressed her naked body close to me. But, as I've been telling you, it was my first case as an op for the Triple-I and I pulled away. I soon learned better.

"They'll have to pay the insurance," I told Mac Brady. "It may need an exhumation and an autopsy, but I'll bet the final report is cardiac failure."

"Yeah," he said.

"All this other stuff is salad," I told him. "A guy died from natural causes and his insurance company gets nicked. T.S. But the other stuff has been interesting."

Suddenly my head began to balloon as I thought of all the threads I had unraveled, all the lies I had listened to, all the motives I had probed.

"And I solved it in two days," I boasted.

Mac Brady looked up at me, dead-pan.

"What took you so long?" he said.

The Case of the Missing Nude

Every time I think I've figured out the human race and have everyone neatly pigeon-holed as to Basic Types, Fundamental Motives and Essential Passions, along comes a case that sticks a knife in the jugular of the Lannihan System. Then I go back to my original belief that all human beings are contrary and unpredictable, and all human desires and emotions are a great big can of worms, with no beginning and no end.

What inspires this melancholy observation is a case I was assigned to in south New Jersey. Actually, there was some argument in the Manhattan offices of the International Insurance Investigators as to whether this particular clambake should be handled by the New York District or the Philadelphia District.

Lt. Gen. Lemuel K. Davidson, USMC (Ret.), the boss of the Triple-I, settled the whole fracas by remarking, somewhat testily, "Lannihan, get cracking." Twenty-four hours later I was holed up in a motel on the outskirts of Shavelton in south Jersey, It was the kind of place where on Saturday night, for excitement, practically the entire population went out and stood alongside the highway and watched the traffic.

Our client in this case was the Arcana Insurance Co. They were holding a two-million-dollar policy on the art collection of a certain Col. Fazely Miller, a retired military type who lived in a rambling estate a few miles outside Shavelton. The art collection was insured against theft, fire and other forms of damage, and the premiums were hefty. Under terms of the policy, the insurance ran only for two-year periods. At the end of each period, before the policy was renewed, Arcana had the right to bring in their own art expert, if they so desired, to inspect the collection and make certain all was copasetic.

Arcana had done exactly that, about two weeks before the Triple-I was called into the case, and the expert had discovered that the gem of the collection, a brilliant Matisse nude, was missing. It had been replaced on the library wall of Colonel Miller's residence with a very clever copy.

Miller claimed the robbery and substitution had been made during the two-year insured period, and he was screaming for $600,000—the appraised value of the painting in question. Arcana wasn't about to dish out a sum like this until they did a little digging and tried to find out where the original Matisse went, who made the copy and who made the substitution.

So there I was in Shavelton, watching the trucks roar by on the turnpike. Gee, it was exciting.

Like the good little gumshoe I am, I had done some digging on the people involved before I headed south through the Lincoln Tunnel. Col. Fazely Miller, I discovered, was a retired U.S. Army man, a West Point graduate who had seen service in several wars as chief of various quartermaster depots. He wasn't exactly a hell-for-leather Patton type. After reading his service record, which Lieutenant General Davidson dredged up for me, I saw that the U.S. Army thought it best, in times of hostilities, to keep him doling out combat boots and jockstraps in such places as Bear's Eye, Nebraska, and Ox Elbow, Louisiana. The Colonel was now 68 and retired. Since the age of 34, he had been married to the former Louisa May Brighton of

Baltimore, Maryland. They had one child, a son.

You've probably read about this son, Capt. Harry Miller. At the time of this case, we were two years into the Vietnam madness and Captain Harry had already won enough medals to make him list to port when he walked. Even if the newspaper reports were only half-right, he was the fightingest man the U.S.A. had produced since Sergeant York. Several times he stormed Viet Cong bunkers by himself, carrying an armload of satchel charges and grenades, and once he was credited with saving his platoon (when he was a lieutenant) by manning a heavy machine gun when all his men had been put out of action and didn't care whether school kept or not. Quite a man, this Capt. Harry Miller.

He was married to Cynthia Howe, formerly of Grand Rapids, Michigan, and she also lived in Colonel Miller's mansion, outside of Shavelton.

So now the stage is set. Enter eager Wolf Lannihan, armed with his great and wonderful knowledge of human beings, their vices and their virtues, their dreams and their greeds, how they respond to temptation and how they react under stress. Feh!

301

The Colonel's house was pleasant and rambling, and so was the Colonel's lady who pushed past the housekeeper (who had answered the doorbell) and welcomed me personally.

I guessed Louisa Miller was in her early 60s. A heavy-set, lumpish, comfortable woman with ready smile and tiny red veins running through the upper parts of her cheeks like vague road maps. I judged she was not a stranger to the sherry bottle. Some local hairdresser had gone out of his mind trying to tint her hair a nice blue-white and arrange it in carefully coiffed curls. She kept poking at it as she kept up a practically nonstop babble, but I could tell from the condition of the ridiculous printed cotton dress she was wearing that, whatever her other vices might be, vanity was not one of them.

She conducted me through the Miller home, explaining that the Arcana Insurance Co. had alerted them to my arrival. The Colonel was out on his morning canter. I already knew the Colonel had inherited money, which explained the art collection and the three-horse stable behind the main house.

What I really wasn't prepared for was the size and diversity of the Colonel's art collection. The paintings and prints were every-where—on the walls of entranceway, living room, library, dining room, along the stairway leading to the upper floor and, presumably, in every bedroom and, for all I knew, in every john in the joint. Great glowing canvases, bursting with color. I'm no art expert but even little old ignorant me could enjoy this stuff and realize it meant years of careful selection and investment.

I could understand a military man buying paintings like *The Charge of the Light Brigade* and *Napoleon Dragging His Ass Back from Moscow* and stuff like that. But most of these paintings were light, graceful, colorful, airy. You know—ballet dancers and nudes and country scenes and even some modern abstracts. Somehow, none of it matched up with the vision I had already formed of the Quartermaster Colonel, the martinet who had devoted his life to getting recruits into uniforms that didn't fit.

After we wandered around for almost an hour, and Mrs. Miller had shown me the spot over the mantel in the well-stocked library where the Matisse had hung, she murmured some excuse and went wandering off. I guessed she was heading for her own room and the sherry bottle, or maybe the pantry and the giant economy-size bottle of vanilla extract.

For a few moments I stared at the blank space where the fake nude had been. The Arcana experts had taken the copy away for infrared analysis, to see if they could determine how long ago, and by whom, the substitution had been made.

I could hear subdued chatter and laughter coming from back rooms—the kitchen area—but no one bothered me. So I took Mrs. Miller at her word. She had said, "Please do make yourself at home." So I made myself at home. I wandered around the main floor, familiarized myself with the layout. Then I climbed the stairs to the second floor, giving the paintings another look. I strolled along the upstairs corridor, opening doors at random and peeking in. I spotted what I figured was the master bedroom, a huge chamber painted a light tint of pink and decorated with steel engravings. Twin beds.

Then there was another large bedroom, probably the resting place of Capt. Harry Miller, when he was home, and his wife Cynthia. This was a pleasant room. No paintings on the walls but plenty of photographs in silver frames scattered about.

Then I opened the door to what looked

like an artist's studio . . . taboret, easel, plenty of brushes and paints. The original windows had been removed and a huge, slanted skylight inserted into the outside wall. The room was an aquarium of light. The half-finished canvas on the easel looked familiar to me. I realized it was a copy of that Rembrandt the Metropolitan had paid more than two million bucks for. A good copy, too. Interesting.

I wandered down to the end of the hall and opened the last door. Boy! It was a kind of solarium, half-room, half-porch. Between the inside and outside areas was a division of sliding glass doors, now thrown back. There was nothing but diaphanous white nylon curtains, billowing gently in the breeze, between the indoor area and the outdoor sundeck. I got a quick impression of white-painted wood furniture—chairs and a flat couch—outside on the deck. Then I saw the woman staring at me through the frosted curtains.

She was seated sideways on a bentwood chair, her naked back exposed to the still-hot September sun. She was wearing some kind of a ruffled white cotton bathing suit she had shrugged off her shoulders and pulled down in front. Way down in front. Her reddish-brown hair was shoulder-length, curled up in feathery wisps. I got a fast look at a strong, expressionless face, brown eyes regarding me gravely. No fear at suddenly discovering a stranger in her home. Obviously, this was Cynthia Miller, young wife of man-of-war Captain Miller.

"I beg your pardon," I called loudly, and began to back out.

"Wait a minute," she said. A strong voice but flat and emotionless.

She tugged up the frilled bodice of the bathing suit, stood and came through the curtains into the inner room. If Captain Harry had known what I was thinking at that moment, he'd have jammed a satchel charge down my throat.

A small woman but with a posture and dignity that made her seem taller . . . high cheekbones . . . a full but firm mouth . . . steady, level eyes . . . wide, creamy shoulders . . . an incredibly narrow waist . . . firm hips and thighs . . . good, straight legs . . . small, strong feet. A woman who needed a lot of man—one man. One good man.

I explained who I was and what I was doing in her home. She introduced herself and held out her hand, not at all embarrassed or seemingly even aware that I had seen her half-naked. Her hand was firm and dry.

There was a robe tossed over a chair in the inner room but she didn't bother putting it on. She sat down, crossed her naked legs, thigh-high, and took the cigarette I offered her. I asked her if we could talk for a moment, and she nodded.

Of course, she knew about the substitution of the Matisse nude. No, she was not aware when the switch had been made. The Colonel had a great number of very beautiful paintings, but though she lived with them and enjoyed them, she couldn't say from day to day which paintings were actually there and which were missing. It made sense to me.

"You're a painter yourself?" I asked her.

"Once I thought I might be," she said levelly, her gaze locked into mine. "But I just don't have it. Now I just copy for my own amusement. I have a studio down the hall. I'm sure you've seen it."

"Yes," I admitted, "and you're very good."

"Good at copying," she said. "I can't create. It's a problem for you, isn't it, Mr. Lannihan?"

I wasn't about to play games with her.

"Yes, it's a problem," I acknowledged. "A very valuable painting has been stolen and a very expert copy left in its place. In the house where this happened lives a very expert painter who does copies. Sure, that's a problem."

"You think I did it?"

"I don't think anything—at the moment. I'm just trying to learn what's happening and what's been going on."

"Do you want me to say I didn't do it?"

I looked at her a long, silent moment. God, she was luscious. I could see the sunshine glinting on the fine golden hairs on her calves and thighs. Her breasts were high and hard. That full mouth was wet and half-parted.

"Yes," I said, in a strangled voice. "I want you to say you didn't do it."

"I didn't do it," she said in a whisper that seemed to have a mocking overtone.

We sat there and stared at each other. Have you ever stared at a woman, your eyeballs linked, both of you wordless—and then the emotional climate changes? You start out strangers, and just by staring at each other, not saying a word, something begins to grow and grow and grow, and finally you're both breathing a little more heavily than you should, and you know—you *know*—that if you ask, "Yes?" she'll say, "Yes."

Sometimes those moments happen.

But it didn't happen this time. I heard the thud of a horse's hooves outside, the shout of the rider, and I rose swiftly, thanked her for her time and hurried downstairs. I was seated casually in the living room leafing through an old copy of *Town & Country*, when Mrs. Miller entered a bit unsteadily, leading by the hand Col. Fazely Miller, clad in jodhpurs and tweed jacket, back from his morning canter, the perfect picture of a retired cavalry colonel. Except that this guy had spent the war years signing invoices for shipments of "Trays, mess, partitioned, stainless steel."

Think of all the clichés about retired military men you've ever read, and you'll get a good mental picture of Col. Fazely Miller. Medium height . . too heavy, but with a flat gut that made me think he might be wearing a corset . . . wisps of grey hair combed sideways across his scalp to conceal his baldness . . . light blue, surprisingly weak eyes . . . a big scabbard of a nose . . . thin lips . . . a receding chin. He must have been much heavier when he bought that jacket: the tweed hung from his shoulders in ugly folds. There were worn leather patches on the elbows.

He offered me a drink, and I accepted gratefully. It was a very thin sideboard indeed. In fact, as far as I could see, there was a bottle of bourbon, a bottle of gin and a bottle of sherry. That was it. I took the bourbon. He poured it into a spotted glass. No offer of ice, soda or water. No effort to find out what his wife might want. She waited hopefully for a moment. Then, when it was obvious she was going drinkless, she tip-toed from the room.

I took him through the whole thing and learned nothing new. He had no idea when the original Matisse had been stolen and the copy substituted. He had so many paintings he couldn't possibly be expected to check every one of them every day. He wasn't even aware of the robbery until the art expert from Arcana had told him.

Yes, it was true his daughter-in-law was an expert copier, but naturally, no one could possibly suspect *her*.

I asked him about the servants. There was one live-in combination cook-housekeeper. A cleaning woman came twice a week. A groundsman-groom came once a week. That was a surprise. I'd have figured a place that size would need at least three or four full-time servants.

There didn't seem much else to say. His flat, blue eyes followed my movements as I drained the warm bourbon, rose and started for the door. He didn't offer me another drink. I paused at the doorway.

"What do you hear from your son, Colonel?" I asked casually.

He waited a long moment.

"I believe he's earned another medal," he said in a voice so cold and emotionless that it shivered me.

Before I left, I took a turn around the grounds. I figured the Colonel might be watching me from a window, but I didn't give a damn. One warm bourbon didn't entitle him to any consideration.

I saw some things I hadn't noticed before. A stable for three horses, but only one stall was occupied and the nag looked somewhat the worse for wear. Slates missing from the roof of the main house. The sidings needed a good coat of paint. The trees and shrubbery needed trimming. There were bald patches on the front lawn. The open front gate, a nice design in wrought iron, was rusted and one hinge was broken.

I got into my ancient Pontiac and drove

back to Shavelton. I was staying in the only motel in town—a place called, believe it or not, The Pleasant Palace. Well, it wasn't a palace but it was surprisingly pleasant, clean and adequately air-conditioned. There was also a combination bar-restaurant.

I went up to my room, dug out my traveling bottle of Jim Beam and ordered up some ice. I was halfway through my first drink before I got the strength to kick off my shoes and flop on the bed and do some thinking. I thought about how Cynthia Miller looked when I first saw her—sitting half-naked on the white chair, the glow of her flesh coming through the billowing white curtain.

I knew that in a small town like this, with one bank, I'd get nowhere. So I called our Manhattan office and told them to run a credit check on Col. Fazely Miller, working through our bank contacts in New York.

I called Arcana and spoke to their Claims Department director. He gave me the number of the art expert who was examining the copy of the Matisse nude that had been substituted for the real thing. He said he'd call the expert and tell him to relay to me anything he had discovered.

I waited 15 minutes to give the Arcana

man a chance to clear me, meanwhile pour-
ing another jolt of Beam elixir. Then I called
the art expert. Like most experts he hemmed
and hawed, afraid to say anything definite.
Finally I got him to admit that, after examining other copies of paintings by Cynthia
Miller, he felt "in all probability," the copy
of the Matisse nude had not been done by
Cynthia.

I asked him if he had any idea who might
have done the copy. He said there were several forgers in this country capable of such
an excellent copy, and many more overseas.
Thanks a lot, I thought—for nothing.

I slept a few hours, had a shower, dressed
and went downstairs for food. I had a reasonably edible steak, two bottles of Heineken
and was on my second brandy when the
waiter told me there was a call from New
York waiting for me.

It was a credit check on Colonel Miller.
Very interesting. He had retired in good
shape, what with his pension and what he
had inherited in blue-chip securities. But then
he had suddenly gotten a vision of himself as
a financial wizard and had started finagling
with stocks, buying short for the most part.
It had taken him almost five years but he
had succeeded in running his nut into a shell.

In other words, the Colonel was hurting. Five live-in servants became one. Three horses became one. The Miller estate began to go to seed. Sad. Very sad.

I'm a romantic, and generally I like military types—even those in the Quartermaster Corps. So I drank more than I should have, but at least I had the sense to stop in good time and go to bed early. I guess I had slept an hour or so when a rapping on my door brought me awake. I padded over in my shorts. All right, I sleep in my underwear. Big deal.

I opened the door. It was Cynthia Miller.

"I didn't do it," she said.

I groaned.

"May I come in?" she asked.

I pulled on a pair of pants (I told you I was a romantic) and built us a couple of Beams with the chips of ice floating around in the warmed bucket. As I came more awake, she began to look better and better to me.

She was wearing a simple black dress that looked like a slip. It had two narrow shoulder straps, was fitted tightly across her breasts and then flared out to mini-length. Her tanned legs were bare. She was wearing leather sandals. I wanted to kiss her toes. I'm nuts for toes.

We both took deep gulps of our drinks, and I said, "I know you didn't do it. He did it. The Colonel. But why? He must have known we'd suspect you—an expert copier. Did he want to hurt you?"

"No," she said. "Not me, Harry."

I didn't get it at first.

"Captain Harry?" I asked. "His hero son? He figured to hit at Harry by implicating you? I know he was hurting for cash. The place is running down. He's got debts. So why didn't he sell off some of his paintings? Why did he have to do it this way?"

"That's the way he is," she said. "He had the Matisse nude copied by a man in San Francisco. I recognized the style. I studied with the man. Then he probably sent the original abroad to be sold. He figured I'd be blamed for it."

"I understand," I said, not understanding at all. "But why you? You say he didn't want to hurt you. Only his son. Why should he want to hurt his son?"

"Were you in the service?"

"Yes."

"The Army has been the Colonel's whole life. But he spent it in quartermaster depots.

315

He was really a clerk. He dealt with uniforms and equipment and hardware. That's what the Army told him to do, and he did it. I think they knew what they were doing. But he had this vision of himself, this dream. A fighting man. A hero. Single-handed charges against the enemy. Medals. He never got a medal. Then his son did everything he had dreamed about all his life. He was jealous. He needed money, and he figured he could steal the Matisse himself. If the insurance company didn't spot the substitution, he'd have the money. If they did, and he could pin it on me, he'd still have the insurance money and somehow he'd cut his son down to size, because he had proved his son's wife was a thief."

"That's crazy," I said.

"Yes," she nodded sadly. "And so is Col. Fazely Miller."

See what I mean about trying to figure out human beings and classify them and assign them to types and pigeon holes? You think you know what makes people tick, and then they upset all your great theories, and you acknowledge that, really, you don't know a damned thing about them.

"All right," I said tiredly. "You give me the name and address of that art forger in

San Francisco, and we'll check it out, and I suppose we'll finally prove Colonel Miller swiped his own Matisse. Everything will be hushed up, and his insurance will be canceled and no one will go to jail. Miller will keep losing money in the stock market, and Mrs. Miller will keep soaking up sherry, and the Miller estate will become the Shavelton version of Skid Row. What a waste. Of everybody's time and everybody's concern."

She didn't say anything.

"What hurts most," I went on, "is your husband. Doing his job and putting his neck on the line every day."

"Yes," she said dully, "just to prove he's a better man than his father is. My husband is a West Point graduate, too. He knows his father's record. What do you think is driving *him?*"

I got sore then.

"Forget it," I yelled at her. "I don't want to hear any more about fathers who collect art and sons who try to get killed and mothers who drink sherry. Right now, I'm sick of people. I'm sick of human beings. I'm going to buy a dog or a cat. I can't stand this mixed-up mess of motives and desires and ambitions and all that. I just don't want to hear any more about it."

She floated out of her chair and came toward me slowly, pulling one strap down from her shoulder. She had this all-over tan, the skin soft and creamy.

"And that's another thing," I yelled at her. "I saw plenty of guys get those 'Dear John' letters. You don't really think I'm going to bed with a woman whose husband is neck-deep in crap overseas, do you? Is that the kind of man you think I am?"

"Whatever might have been between Harry and me was over a long time before he went overseas," she said slowly. "I was ready to leave for Reno when his orders came, and then he went to Vietnam, and I didn't feel right about it. So legally I'm still his wife. Legally. But not morally or personally. And he knows it. He never writes to me, and I never write to him. The only thing in his life is proving that he's a better man than his father."

"I don't give a damn about that," I said angrily. "I don't care what your motives are, or what his are, or what your relations are. All I know is that I'm not going to touch you."

I told you I was a romantic, didn't I? I'm also a liar.

The publishers hope that this
Large Print Book has brought
you pleasurable reading.
Each title is designed to make
the text as easy to see as possible.
G.K. Hall Large Print Books
are available from your library and
your local bookstore. Or, you can
receive information by mail on
upcoming and current Large Print Books
and order directly from the publishers.
Just send your name and address to:

G.K. Hall & Co.
70 Lincoln Street
Boston, Mass. 02111

or call, toll-free:

1-800-343-2806

A note on the text
Large print edition designed by
Bernadette Montalvo.
Composed in 18 pt Plantin
on a Xyvision 300/Linotron 202N
by Genevieve Connell
of G.K. Hall & Co.